Stretched Thin

SVR Files

#1

Amber Gabriel

Presented by H. L. Burke

This is a work of fiction. Similarities to real people, places, or events are entirely coincidental.

STRETCHED THIN
First edition. February 22, 2025.
Copyright © 2025 Amber Gabriel.
Written by Amber Gabriel.

All rights reserved.
Cover art by K. M. Carroll
Cover layout by Jennifer Hudzinski

The Supervillain Rehabilitation Project (AKA SVR-Verse or DOSA-Verse) is a multi-series superhero universe (currently) consisting of four separate series.

Series One: Supervillain Rehabilitation Project

The first series from a timeline perspective, this series follows superheroine, Prism, as she attempts to redeem her late father's legacy by helping his disgraced protege get back on the hero path.

Relapsed (Short Story Prequel)
Reformed
Redeemed
Reborn
Refined
Reunion

Series Two: Supervillain Rescue Project

This Young Adult spin-off takes place after the main series when Prism and Fade start a camp for at risk superpowered teens and follows three new superpowered characters, Jake, Laleh, and Marco.

Power On
Power Play
Power Through
Power Up

Series Three: Supervillain Romance Project
This series follows the Park family, a separate superhero clan, as they fight villains—and sometimes date them. This series can be read independently, though later books feature crossover characters from the YA and Original Series.
Blind Date with a Supervillain
On the Run with a Supervillain
Captured by a Supervillain
Engaged to a Supervillain
Accidentally a Supervillain

Series Four: Superhero Romance Project
While there are some cameos from other series, this is a series of standalone romantic comedies featuring other superpowered characters from the universe and can be read independently.
A Superhero for Christmas
A Superhero Ever After
Second Chance Superhero
Wishing on a Supervillain
Her Fake Superhero Boyfriend
Rescuing a Supervillain
Courting a Superhero

Series Five: Supervillain Legacy Project
Set seventeen years after the original series, this YA series features children of the original series as well as other new young characters.
Game On
Game Changer

Anthology: The DOSA Files, Tales from the SVR Universe
Stories by multiple writers set within the world of the SVR. Stories are not necessarily canon to the universe as a whole.
Volume I, II, & III

The SVR Files:
The Supervillain Rehabilitation Project Universe expands with this new collection of titles, produced via H.L. Burke with collaboration from other writers.
Stretched Thin by Amber Gabriel

Chapter One

Elam flipped a switch, and the neon sign buzzed and glowed, declaring the bar open for business. He stared out the window at a mirage on the pavement. Patrons would soon be lining up for a cold drink, ready to escape the desert heat.

Most of them would be locals. Tourists tended to stick close to the casinos, and Thirsty"s sat right on the edge of Reno city limits. But lately ... Elam's presence had been attracting some unwanted attention.

Thirsty"s keys jingled as he unlocked the door. A dusty pickup pulled into the parking lot, followed by a sedan with a duct-taped fender and a rusty Camaro. "Looks like today will be a busy day."

Elam nodded, noting the wariness beneath his employer"s cheerful tone. He slid onto a stool behind a desk near the door as Thirsty shuffled over to the bar. Hopefully, it would be an uneventful day as well.

The door opened, and the first customer entered. "Hello, Elam." A white-haired man in a plaid shirt and overalls raised a hand.

Elam stretched his hand across the desk without walking around and gave him a high-five. "Hey, Ronny. How's it going?"

"Can't complain. You need to work out though. You're getting flabby." Ronny laughed at his own joke.

Elam's arm snapped back to its natural shape, and he smiled as if he hadn't heard the same line nearly every day for the past three months. Having a regular job was weird, though it was kind of nice to have people recognize and be glad to see him.

"My man." A dark-skinned man in a Lakers jersey clasped Elam's hand as he entered. "What'd you think of that game last night?"

"Pretty exciting. I missed the end though." He'd been busy.

The man leaned closer and raised an eyebrow. "Oh, yeah? I heard there was some excitement here after I left last night."

"Yeah." Elam grimaced and squirmed in his seat. "Had to call the cops."

"Aww, I bet you had that punk tied up in a bow for 'em."

"Pretty much."

"Don't let him fool you, Dion," said a gray-bearded man in a flat cap. "He had him wound up tighter than a spool of thread. Looked like something out of a cartoon."

Dion turned around. "And how would you know, old man? You're snoring in your bed before the sun goes down."

"I saw it on video." The bearded man held up his phone.

"You saw it on the 'Tok?" Dion guffawed. "Man, this place gettin' too popular for me. Let's get some seats while we still can."

The three men took seats at the bar, trading jokes with Thirsty and ribbing each other lightheartedly. Two elderly ladies, one with a walker, came in and sat at the video poker machines. Elam slouched against the back of his seat. He looped his thumbs through his jeans and wondered if asking Thirsty for a pink shirt had been a bad idea. The bright bubblegum tee with Bouncer in black lettering, his only homage to his former supervillain identity, served as a reminder to the public of his identity as well. Everyone knew where to find him, which was becoming problematic.

A compact car with the logo of a local news station drove into the parking lot. Two men climbed out and got a camera and some gear out of the trunk.

Great. Just what we need.

A dapper young man with perfectly styled hair and a neat polo sailed through the door followed by a grungy dude hefting a camera. The reporter honed in on Elam immediately.

"Are you Elam Bentley, formerly the Rubber Bandit?"

Elam held out a hand with his most business-like manner. "Let me see some IDs first."

The news crew handed over their IDs dutifully. Twenty-four and twenty-eight. Too bad he couldn't throw them out.

"I'm Elam Bentley."

The cameraman lifted the camera onto his shoulder, while the reporter held up a microphone. "We'd like to ask you a few questions."

"Now's not really a good time. I've got to watch the door."

The reporter raised an eyebrow and glanced around. "Doesn't look too busy to me."

Before Elam could reply, Thirsty ambled over. "I'm the owner. What do you want to know?"

The reporter nodded at the cameraman and a red light turned on. "What's it like to have a super-abled employee? It's unusual to find them in the private sector."

"He does a good job," said Thirsty firmly. "I don't have to worry about him getting hurt or hurting anybody else."

"Why is that? Are you unable to be injured?" The reporter shoved the microphone in front of Elam's face.

"Umm..."

"Don't you know, this dude is rubber?" Dion sidled over and put his arm across Elam's shoulders. "Even bullets bounce off him."

That wasn't exactly true, but the door opened before Elam could clarify. A mob of preppy girls gathered inside. They looked decidedly out of place on this side of town, which made him suspicious. "IDs please." He stretched his arm across the entry to form a barrier so no one could sneak past. "Give us some room, fellas," the pitch of his voice heightened as his arm lengthened.

Dion obediently backed off, but the cameraman angled toward the newcomers.

"If you will come this way—" Thirsty beckoned the reporter, "—I can answer your questions."

Elam studied the first girl's ID. She had so much makeup on, it was hard to tell her age. The tips of her brown hair had been bleached and dyed blue, but her license matched her height and weight. As a former villain, he'd owned his share of fake IDs, and this one looked legit. He handed it back. "You're good." He retracted his arm to let her pass.

"Is it true that picking a fight with your bouncer has become an initiation rite for local gangs?"

Elam unconsciously rubbed his side as he studied the next girl's license. The guy he'd fought the previous night had sucker-punched him, leaving a mottled bruise that would have been way worse if not for his sable healing factor. Holding his body in a constant state of elasticity was impossible, and he hadn't been prepared. "Go ahead," he told the second girl.

"Well, you'd have to ask the police about that," Thirsty replied. "I don't know anything about any gang ties. All I know is, we don't want any trouble. If anyone causes any, we're calling law enforcement. If you'll excuse me, I got to take orders." Thirsty sidled off, and the camera crew busied themselves taking shots of the interior.

As Elam took the third girl's ID, the last two whispered to each other. One girl, who had a baseball cap pulled low on her forehead, shook her head and motioned toward the camera. The other hissed something at the girl in the cap and stepped forward as Elam waved the third girl through.

The fourth girl's ID was an obvious fake. A good one, but easy to spot if you knew what to look for. "Sorry, miss," Elam extended his flexibility into the plastic and stretched it like taffy, then tied it in a knot, "this one's no good." He handed it back, and it hardened into a permanent loop.

She shrugged and tossed it in the trash can without protest. "It was worth a try." She waved at her three friends who had claimed a table. "I'll wait outside."

That was ... too easy. As Elam held out his hand for the last girl's license, his senses heightened. She avoided his gaze. Her ID looked real, but something was off. "What's your birthday, Tammy?" he asked.

She raised her eyes and stared at him blankly. "Huh?"

"Your birthday?"

"Um ..." She glanced around, and before he could blink, she was across the room, chugging a drink from her friends' table.

Crap. A speed sable. The girl with the fake ID must have loaned the underage sable her license. *Probably some stupid sorority stunt.* Hazing and underage drinking were misdemeanors and had to be reported, or Thirsty's could be liable. He couldn't just let it go. And the kid had powers. That meant calling DOSA, the last people he wanted to involve.

The boss picked up his phone to dial the authorities while Elam's arm shot to the door handle, holding it closed and rubberizing it, just in case. "Tell them we need a disruptor cuff." Maybe the normie police would have a couple on hand for situations like this, and he wouldn't have to deal with DOSA directly.

"Wait, don't call the cops," said the blue-haired girl. She rose, and the others followed. "We're leaving."

The news crew followed the girls with the camera, blocking their view of the door.

"Air that footage, and we'll sue," hissed one of them. "My dad's a lawyer."

"Lacey, get the camera," directed Blue-Hair.

The speed sable hesitated. "Those are expensive. It could be a felony."

"If you're caught, your legal career is toast anyway. You're faster than he is. Come on!"

Lacey disappeared in a blur and snatched the camera from the operator's shoulder. A nanosecond later, she slammed into the door with full force. Lacey's body flew across the room before Elam could catch her. His elongated arm reached her just as she hit the opposite wall. He infused her with his powers to help soften the impact, guiding her limp form to the floor. The camera crunched against the hardwood planks, the red light still blinking.

Should have accounted for the super speed.

Sirens wailed. A yellow sports car sped toward the parking lot exit only to be blocked by three police cruisers. The real Tammy would not get away.

Elam released the door to let the cops worry about the other girls and hurried to Lacey's side. Still connected, he detected a faint heartbeat. The knock against the door would have rattled her brain, but as long as she was alive, her healing factor should take care of the rest. Sensing that becoming momentarily rubber had kept her bones intact, he slowly returned her to normal.

A low whistle alerted him to Ronny's presence. The elderly man lowered himself slowly to kneel beside the prone figure and felt for a pulse. "She's alive, but out cold." He turned around and raised his voice. "Mitch, call the paramedics on that fancy phone of yours."

Elam sank to the floor and leaned against the wall, running his fingers through his sandy hair. He hadn't wanted anyone to get hurt, sable or otherwise, but his pride had kept him from waiting for DOSA. "I should have just let her go," he said, voicing his regret to no one in particular.

"You couldn't predict what would happen," answered Ronny, squeezing his shoulder. "It's not your fault. You weren't the one breaking the law."

A figure blocked the light from the door, and Elam felt a chill. "Don't be too sure about that. I'm certain we can find something to charge you with."

Elam closed his eyes, wishing he could unhear the familiar voice of his nemesis. Byte, the leader of the local DOSA team, had had it in for him ever since he'd been forced to release Elam on a technicality—a technicality caused by his own ineptitude.

"Hey, Byte. Look." Elam recognized the voice of Rightcross, Reno's power sable, and opened his eyes to see her pointing at the unconscious girl. "It's Lacey Greenberg, daughter of that shipping magnate. We're supposed to be keeping tabs on her."

Byte scowled. "Great. Mr. Greenberg's not going to be happy about this." He glared at Elam. "You're in big trouble now."

Elam's anger flared, but before he could respond, Dion stepped up in his defense. "Hey, my man Elam wasn't the one drinking with a borrowed ID." He poked Byte in the chest. "And if you was s'posed to keep tabs on her, how'd she end up here in the first place?"

"Back off, normie," growled Byte. Turning all of his ire on Elam, he put his hands on his hips and continued, "There's laws against the use of excessive force."

Bracing himself against a chair, Ronny slowly stood and arched his back to unkink it. "Technically, she was the one who applied the force since she was the one moving."

Dion raised both eyebrows and waved his arms toward Ronny. "Listen to the man!"

It warmed Elam to hear people come to his defense, but he didn't want his friends—could he call them friends?—to draw Byte's ire. "Thanks guys, but this hero's so bad at paperwork, he couldn't make a charge stick with super glue."

"You—you," Byte sputtered, at a loss for words.

One of the ladies at the poker machines shook her cane at him. "You need to learn some manners, young man." Despite his graying hair, Byte was half her age. Young was relative.

At that moment, a pair of paramedics wheeled in a gurney, and a temporary truce ensued as everyone shifted to make room. A uniformed police officer followed behind them with a notepad.

"Is this the one who caused all the ruckus?" asked the officer, gesturing toward Lacey.

"She's a sable under our supervision," snapped Byte. "We'll take it from here. Rightcross, slap a disruptor cuff on her, and we'll follow the ambulance to the hospital." He pointed at Elam. "This isn't over, villain!" Then he turned and stalked out.

At the mention of the disruptor, Elam ignored Byte and focused on Rightcross. "A disruptor won't affect her ability to heal, will it?"

The lines around Rightcross's eyes softened as she regarded him. She shook her head. "I'll put it on her ankle—that will keep her from using her speed to run when she wakes up, but it shouldn't interfere with her recovery." A lock of pink hair fell across her forehead, and she brushed it out of the way before securing the cuff.

The paramedics completed their exam, transferred Lacey to the stretcher, and wheeled her outside. Rightcross followed, tossing her hair at the reporter's raised cell phone as she passed. Her breezy, shoulder-length waves matched the color of Elam's shirt.

The camera operator retrieved his device and inspected it.

"Does it still work?" asked the reporter, still holding up his cell.

"The lens is cracked, and this panel is broken, but it's still recording. Man, that'll be some awesome footage."

"Mr. Bentley," the reporter pointed his phone at Elam, "Do you feel the role of bouncer permits you to act in place of law enforcement?"

Elam blinked, unsure how to respond.

"Do you agree that preventing customers from exiting a building is equivalent to kidnapping?"

"What?" Elam was incredulous at this line of questioning. "No!"

"Comment," interrupted Thirsty, inserting himself between them. "He has no comment. Time to go." He herded the news crew out the door, ignoring the reporter's continued prodding.

As soon as they had gone, more police entered and started their own round of questioning. By the time everyone had given their statement, night had fallen. The customers filed out, yawning and bleary eyed.

"We got our money's worth of entertainment tonight, didn't we, Bett?" said the lady with the cane.

"We sure did," responded Bett, leaning on her walker. "We'll be back tomorrow!"

"Don't worry about what that DOSA fellow said." Ronny patted Elam on the back. "The police didn't seem to think you'd done anything wrong. Keep a stiff upper lip."

Elam smiled, but just because he'd avoided arrest today didn't mean he was completely in the clear. He could face civil charges if any of the girls' families took exception to his actions. His faith in the justice system was weaker than Byte's lame tech powers.

Elam switched off the "open" sign. Thirsty locked the door with a sigh. They cleaned up and washed the few glasses that had been used and headed toward the employee entrance in the back.

"I think, Elam, you might oughta lay low for a while."

Elam's heart sank at Thirsty's words. However, he couldn't argue with the wisdom of them. He swallowed. "I suppose so."

"I can call Luis to fill in for a few days."

Elam nodded, his throat tight. He feared the days would stretch into weeks. Maybe it would be better for Thirsty if he didn't come back at all.

"It's not your fault people keep trying to test you. You've done a good job."

"Thanks. Thanks for giving me a chance." At least he'd kept Thirsty from losing his liquor license. Fat lot of good that would do him if he was no longer employed. "See you around."

"I'll be in touch," Thirsty replied. But Elam knew he wouldn't.

Chapter Two

Back in his motel room, Elam lay on his bed, staring at the smoke-stained popcorn ceiling. He'd turned off the TV after the second news cycle.

Bouncer bounces coed against a wall. Local hero calls for charges against former villain.

Newscasters and anchors analyzed his actions, most painting him as some sort of egomaniac who got a kick out of beating up little girls, "former villain" being the kindest term used. Footage of the door as the camera flew backward played on a loop.

Lacey's family managed to keep her name out of the story. The video of her was blurry and didn't show her face. He hoped that same fear of publicity would keep them from pursuing charges against him. While no legal action would be taken against Thirsty's, it looked like the girls would get away with their little stunt.

This is what I get for trying to go straight. Not that he'd had much choice. With Byte breathing down his neck, he'd been unable to retreat to his lair and access his spare cash. Food and lodging ate up most of his meagre earnings. He had a couple thousand bucks from a reward for recovering some stolen goods, but that wouldn't last him long.

Now that his name and face were known, he could no longer commit crimes as the Rubber Bandit. Though they'd failed to convict him, Byte and Rightcross had accomplished that much. A new villain popping up with his same skill set would be just as obvious. No, he'd have to find another legitimate job. But who would hire him?

Eventually, he drifted off to sleep, only to be startled awake a few hours later by a knock on his door. Elam peered through the peephole and recognized Officer Fang, the man who had ensured he received the reward money and helped him land the job at Thirsty's. His relief at it not being a reporter quickly changed to apprehension.

"Hello, Fang," he said as he opened the door. "Here to arrest me?"

"Not today. May I come in?"

Elam stepped aside to let the man enter. Only then did he notice the officer wore plain clothes. "Is this a social call? I don't have any snacks."

"What? Oh." Fang smoothed his brown suit coat. "No, I've been promoted to detective."

"Congratulations."

"Thank you."

After an awkward pause, Elam motioned Fang into one of the room's two chairs while he sat in the other. "So, what can I do for you, detective?"

"I'm hoping we can help each other."

"How so?"

"I've been assigned to the Youth Gang Task Force. The Bandidos de Goma gang has been expanding its territory. Recruiting new members and edging out rival groups." Fang leaned forward and rested his elbows on his knees. "It looks like they're trying to establish a presence in Las Vegas."

Elam rubbed his eyes. "And what am I supposed to do about that? I don't have any gang ties. I've only run with other supervillains, and I haven't exactly kept in touch. Besides, everyone knows I've gone straight. I mean, my cover is kind of blown."

"But that's what makes you perfect for this job," Fang insisted.

Elam raised an eyebrow. "You're not making any sense. Just what do you want me to do?"

"Look, you had no option but to take a legitimate job, but you didn't go with DOSA. You were a bouncer. A tough guy. You went with something familiar and suited to your particular talents."

"So? Nothing wrong with that."

"Of course not. But it sends a signal that you haven't taken sides. You're still open to being a villain if the opportunity presents itself. Why do you think so many crazies have shown up at Thirsty's lately? It's not a coincidence."

An uncomfortable feeling settled over Elam, making his skin prickle. "What do you mean?"

"The guy who picked a fight with you two days ago? He was recently recruited by the Bandidos."

So, the reporter was right about one thing, thought Elam as he repressed a shudder. He didn't like being messed with.

"And those girls yesterday?"

"Yeah? Don't tell me they have gang connections."

Fang nodded slowly. "One of them was de Goma's daughter."

Elam leaned back in his chair in surprise. "Not Lacey? I thought her name was Greenberg."

"No, the daughter's name was Julia."

"The one with the blue hair." He remembered reading her name on her ID. But her last name was Diaz, not de Goma. "Why?"

"To see how you would handle another sable. Julia persuaded Lacey to join her sorority. Fed her some nonsense about it being good for her resume. Then talked her into coming to the bar."

Anger surged through Elam's veins. He hated being manipulated. Hated that Lacey had inadvertently gotten hurt. Knowing they'd brought her to the bar because of him made him feel even worse.

"Are any of them going to face charges?"

Fang sighed. "Unfortunately, no. We got most of the story out of Lacey, but she refuses to press charges against the other girls for hazing, which they all deny anyway. The local DOSA team, with whom you are familiar, ran interference with the hospital staff and wouldn't let anyone take Lacey's blood alcohol level, so we don't have anything on her for the underage drinking other than eyewitness accounts. Thirsty isn't anxious to follow up with that, so the whole thing is a wash. Except for you."

"Yeah, I'm out of a job." Elam crossed his arms in disgust.

"Not for long. I have a feeling the Bandidos will be sending a recruiter to talk to you."

It took a moment for Fang's statement to sink in. "So," he drew out the word, "you want me to say yes."

"We need someone on the inside. So far, we haven't been able to infiltrate this gang."

Elam shook his head. "I don't do guns. I'm not a druggie or a dealer. I don't think I'm a good fit."

"You won't have to deal or carry a gun. With all the sables running around, gangs want security with superpowers to protect them from heroes and supervillain syndicates. The government has to combat the huge rise in overdoses, which means all law enforcement agencies will be working together more closely, even DOSA. Criminal organizations want to be prepared."

"So, say I accept a position as a glorified bodyguard for de Goma or whatever. Number one—" Elam held up a finger, "—what do you want me to do, and number two, how do I keep myself alive and out of jail?"

"That's three things."

"Whatever. I need some answers before I agree to this hypothetical nonsense."

"Our ultimate goal is to compile enough damning evidence against Julio de Goma that we can lock him in a cell and throw away the key. We don't even have concrete proof connecting him to his public persona. And anything we can do to cause a major disruption in his supply chain is a plus. We'll work out a system for you to let us know when you want to talk. I've got a lead on an animal charmer. We'll be able to communicate without the Bandidos catching on."

"So that answers my first question. What about the jail part?"

"DOSA will be helping us out with that."

Elam frowned. "I don't want to work with DOSA." Though he wouldn't mind seeing the look on Byte's face when he found out they'd be on the same side.

"That's the only catch." Fang spread out his arms, palms up. "You have to work with them. The only way I can keep you out of jail if you join the Bandidos is to employ you, and as a sable, DOSA is the only agency who will take you without prior qualifications or extensive training."

Elam groaned. "There has to be another way. Can't I just be an informant?"

"You could, but you'd have less protection and considerably less pay. I can't guarantee anything. With DOSA, you'll just be a short-term contractor. You can leave when the job is finished. No immunity from prosecution for past or future crimes, though."

Elam stood and paced the worn and garishly patterned carpet. "How long do I have to decide?"

"Until you accept a job with the Bandidos."

Elam ran his fingers through his hair and glanced furtively toward the door. "I suppose they're already watching me. How will I explain you being here?"

Detective Fang stood. "I'm just tying up some loose ends from yesterday. As far as the public knows, I'm just a regular police detective. Only a few people in my precinct know I'm on the task force. De Goma has a long reach, so just my immediate superiors have been read in." He paused a beat before continuing. "The local DOSA office won't be in the loop either."

Elam let that sink in. "So that means ... Byte will still be breathing down my neck. Which will look normal. They're bound to muck things up, regardless, so I suppose it's good I can still do my best to annoy him." He rubbed his stubbly chin. He should probably make himself presentable before the Bandidos decided to pick him up.

Fang walked to the door and turned, pulling a paper from his coat pocket. "If you decide to go all in, scan this QR code and fill out the forms it takes you to. Then tear up the paper and delete your scanner and browser history."

Elam took the paper. "And if I don't?"

"Tear it up anyway. You don't want the gang getting hold of it."

Fang let himself out, and Elam stared at the closed door. After a split second debate, he walked swiftly to the table and sat down to complete the online forms. Except for his pride, it didn't hurt anything to fill them out. Though flattered that Fang trusted him enough to let him in on the assignment, signing the forms didn't turn him into one of the good guys. He could always entertain a better offer.

Chapter Three

Less than six hours later, Elam sat in the back of a black Suburban wedged between two muscly, tattooed menaces. When they'd knocked on his door, they had very politely and stereotypically asked him to take a ride. Even if Fang hadn't given him a heads-up, he'd had enough experience with villains to play it cool.

They headed toward the ritzy side of town, passed into a gated community, then through another gate into a private residence. Rock gardens, cultivated cacti, and tropical plants decorated the landscaping, and surrounding the house itself was a small lawn—probably the only real grass in town outside the golf course.

The goons on either side of him got out, and he followed them up the steps and into a spacious, two-story entryway. Elam glanced up the stairs and saw Julia leaning against the railing sipping from a martini glass. She watched him, expressionless, her face a mask of heavy eyeshadow and mascara.

Goon One walked to a set of thick, wooden double doors on one side of the entry and rapped twice with his knuckles. Elam heard a muffled reply. Goon One opened the door and motioned for him to enter. "This way."

To Elam's surprise, inside the study, behind a rich, mahogany desk sat a businesslike man in a fitted black suit and red tie. With neatly combed, short, black hair and hazel eyes, he looked more like a movie star than a gang boss—except for the pair of armed security guards on either side of him. The door to the study closed, the other two goons remaining outside.

"The Rubber Bandit, I presume." He motioned to the chair opposite him. "Take a seat. Normally, my men would search you for weapons, but I suspect that would be as offensive as it would be unnecessary."

"I don't do guns," replied Elam tersely as he slid into an upholstered armchair. "Don't need 'em." The guards narrowed their eyes at him. A younger man, leaning against the wall behind the boss, studied him with curiosity.

"Yes, you have other means of defense. That is why I sent for you." The boss appeared relaxed, speaking without a hint of an accent. "You know who I am?"

This was where Elam had to be careful. Without Fang's warning, he would have had no idea. Even still, he'd never heard of the man before today. He'd Googled him, but de Goma appeared to be a title rather than a formal name, and no photos popped up. The daughter, Julia Diaz, had some social media accounts, but nothing online hinted about gang connections. According to the internet, Julio Diaz owned multiple corporations that no one had ever heard of. The man must have a skilled media team to maintain such a low digital profile.

"No, I'm afraid not."

The boss nodded slowly. "Good. That is good. If you had, I might have had to kill someone." He grinned, and a flash of steel in his eyes sent a chill down Elam's spine. "My name is Julio Diaz. Let's say I'm in the import-export business. I heard you've spent some time in Colombia."

This guy had done his homework. Or, more likely, someone had done it for him. "A little. It's a beautiful country. And I know a guy who does sable enhancements, cheap." Not to mention his Colombian neighbors had practically raised him while his single mother worked three jobs. Hortencia was like a grandmother to him. When her parents died, she'd moved back to her family's *finca* in the Andes where his mother now kept house for her. It eased his mind to know the two people most important to him were far removed from any danger his villainy could pose for them.

"*¿Hablas Español?*" Diaz's polished accent was so pure and American, Elam couldn't detect any regional inflections.

"*Sí. Soy fluido.*" His own accent was decidedly Colombian.

Mr. Diaz raised an eyebrow. "But you have no affiliations with any South American ... associations or syndicates, political or otherwise?"

"No."

Mr. Diaz tapped his fingers on the desk for a moment. Then he leaned back and angled his body to one side. "So then, let's see how effective your enhancements really are. I think it's time for a demonstration."

The young man behind him suddenly straightened, pulled a gun from the small of his back, pointed it directly at Elam's torso, and fired.

At first sight of the weapon, Elam reacted instinctually. His body contorted, bending out of the path of the bullets as the man emptied the magazine into the chair. Elam's arm shot toward the man, wrapping around his hand and turning him to rubber. One of the security guards flinched, and Elam jerked the shooter forward and wrapped him around the first guard like a wet noodle. For good measure, and because he was riled, he grabbed the second guard's gun. Growing a third hand from his elbow, he ejected the magazine, cleared the chamber, and knocked the guard out with his own pistol. He threw the weapon on the floor at his feet and stared at Diaz, panting.

"Well," the gang leader stood and surveyed the room with his hands on his hips, "I must say, you have exceeded my expectations—and in quite an unorthodox fashion." He resumed his seat, waving his hands at the shooter and the other guard. "You can let them go. I think I've seen enough to know what you are capable of. I had thought you could stop bullets without dodging them, but perhaps I was misinformed."

Elam glanced dubiously at the ball of limbs he still grasped and slowly unwound them. His heart pounded so hard, he could see it thumping in his still elasticized chest. Once the two men were separated, he recalled his power and released them. The guard leaned against the wall for support while Elam grabbed and unloaded the remaining guns. The other man slumped to the floor with a groan.

"I'll say you were misinformed," Elam rasped as he caught his breath. "I can turn anything I touch into rubber temporarily, but I have to touch it. Even if it's rubberized, to stop something, its momentum has to be absorbed or redirected—impossible with that many bullets fired point blank."

"I see." Diaz gestured toward the chair Elam had occupied, which now sported several bullet holes in the tan leather. "Many of my furnishings contain ballistic rubber. It can stop bullets, but as you say, it must absorb them. I can understand you not wanting to do that."

Elam glanced at the back side of the chair, which remained pristine. The young man who had shot at him rested a hand on the desk and pulled himself up.

"Meet my son, Angelo." Mr. Diaz turned to the young man, a raised eyebrow the only hint of his concern. "How are you, Angelo?"

Angelo shuddered. "Every muscle in my body aches. Other than that, I'm great."

Elam bared his teeth. "I don't like being shot at."

"Perfectly understandable. But you must forgive Angelo. I wanted to see you in action. With sables becoming more and more common, I feel the need to diversify my staff. I am prepared to offer you a lucrative salary to join my team of personal bodyguards."

"I'm surprised you don't just get the treatment yourself. Plenty of places outside the U.S. have unregulated labs so you wouldn't have to register."

Diaz shook his head. "There are multiple reasons why that is not desirable, the chief of which is that the results can neither be guaranteed nor controlled. One could end up with unwanted effects, if any at all. No, I would much rather know what I am getting."

Both guards had now recovered, though the guns remained at Elam's feet. Elam stood still, half incensed, half amused at the ludicrous situation. If Fang hadn't needed a presence in this organization, he might have walked out.

"So, what do you say?" prompted Diaz.

Elam shrugged and flopped back into the chair. "I suppose so. If the pay is good enough."

"I expect unquestioning loyalty. You will be attached specifically to me, but you will need to coordinate with my head of security on safety protocols." By silent agreement, Angelo and the guards picked up their weapons and reloaded them. "You will need to turn in your electronic devices, including any phones. We will get you a new one."

"What about my personal contacts?"

Diaz glanced at Angelo. "If you have any information you need to retrieve from your phone that is not stored in the cloud, Angelo can supervise you while you copy it down."

"I'd appreciate that." Storing information online meant others could steal it, and he had a few numbers he didn't want to lose. He could brazen out keeping Fang's number. Connections in law enforcement were valuable, even for criminals.

"Any other questions?"

"Are you the only one I need to protect?"

"Ah. I am your primary concern. When my children are with me, you can protect them as well, but everyone else will either aid in our defense or get out of the way."

"One more thing." Elam hesitated, unsure how the gang boss would view his request. "I'd like to visit that girl, Lacey Greenberg, to make sure she's okay."

Diaz leaned forward with his elbow on the desk and rested his chin in his hand. "Why?"

It was a good question. Elam wondered himself. Avoiding collateral damage was good policy but not something he worried about after the fact. He was usually good enough it wasn't an issue. Plus, he'd like to find out if she planned to sue. "Though I might come off a little flippant, I do take pride in my work. As a bouncer, I was supposed to protect people. I failed to take her super speed into account when I rubberized the door, and she rebounded harder than I expected. I won't make that mistake again."

"I should hope not," said Diaz dryly, his voice as cold and hard as a slab of granite. Elam bet he had a low tolerance for mistakes. "But," continued Diaz, "she is a contact I would like to keep." He consulted a legal pad. "She was released this morning, but I can have a driver take you to see her. You can stop at your motel on the way back to pick up your things. I'll settle your bill. Angelo, go with him."

Except for a slight wince when he moved, Angelo led the way from the room as if nothing unusual had occurred. Despite his pretended calm, Elam's adrenaline jitters had not subsided. The mission was already way more dangerous than he'd expected. He wouldn't be able to relax for a second until it was over.

If he survived it.

Chapter Four

Twenty minutes later, the Suburban left the Diaz compound. Angelo, sitting in front with the driver, smiled at Elam in the rear-view mirror. "I hope there's no hard feelings for earlier."

"What, you mean shooting at me? I think we're even."

"Yeah, I feel like I've just competed in an iron man tournament. How long will that last?"

"About as long as it would if you'd really worked your muscles." After a short pause, Elam commented, "You're pretty good with a handgun. You had a nice grouping."

"Well," said Angelo, drawing out the word, "It was pretty close range. But I do practice a lot." He grinned.

"That's apparent." Elam made a mental note that Angelo was susceptible to flattery. He seemed an easy-going kid at the moment—he couldn't be more than twenty, but maybe he just looked younger than Julia due to his lack of cosmetics—but anyone who could empty a pistol into someone, or the place someone was supposed to be, without hesitation, had to border on the insane. He couldn't afford to get complacent around him.

When they pulled up in front of the sorority house just before dusk, Elam almost changed his mind. The Reno DOSA team's black SUV sat right in front. He steeled himself for an unpleasant encounter. After all, he was untouchable now, for a myriad of reasons.

Angelo followed him up the steps. Elam didn't bother to knock but let himself into the large, open front room. Lacey sat with her legs up in a recliner with Rightcross in an adjacent chair. Byte, to Elam's relief, was absent.

Rightcross narrowed her eyes at him. Her purple jumpsuit shimmered as she uncrossed her legs, fitting her just a little too well. "What are you doing here?"

Elam addressed himself to Lacey. "I came to see how you were doing and offer my apologies for how I handled the situation yesterday."

The girl flushed. "I—it was my fault. I knew better than to do something stupid like that. I'm sorry."

Elam perched on the arm of the empty chair on her other side. "How are you?"

"Much better now. I was really sore when I woke up in the hospital last night."

Angelo took a position next to Elam but remained standing. "I know what you mean," he muttered, eying Elam.

Lacey glanced up at Angelo inquisitively.

Angelo grinned. "He gave me a demonstration this afternoon. Tied me up—literally." When Lacey's mouth formed a sympathetic 'O,' he held out his hand with a grin. "I'm Angelo. Julia's brother."

Lacey took his hand and shook it, but her eyes clouded when he mentioned Julia. "I don't suppose she's said anything about my initiation? I don't know if they'll let me stay here now."

Angelo shook his head. "She hasn't mentioned anything to me, but from what I heard, you should have passed."

Rightcross patted Lacey's shoulder. "No one can kick you out of the sorority without admitting to hazing. Don't worry."

Lacey let out a breath of relief and looked up at Elam. "I hope I didn't cause any trouble for the bar owner."

"Nothing long term." Elam gave her a reassuring half-smile.

Lacey sighed. "That's good. I'm still in trouble from my dad. He threatened to bring me home and make me take online courses." She wrinkled her nose. "I'm no good at those."

"But we're going to make sure no one gets you in any more scrapes, so it won't be a problem." Rightcross glared at both men. "She needs to rest. Time for you to go." She stood to shoo them out.

"We're going," said Elam as he rose. "I'm glad to see you are recovering," he told Lacey before turning toward the door. The lack of reference to possible litigation was also a relief.

"It was nice to meet you," Angelo called over his shoulder as he followed.

Once outside, Rightcross clamped her hand on Elam's arm like a vice. Angelo went ahead but paused at the bottom of the steps, close enough to overhear without inserting himself into the conversation.

Rightcross squeezed harder. The strength sable's power would have crushed a lesser man. As it was, Elam allowed his arm to go limp to avoid bruising under the pressure.

"I don't know what you're playing at," she hissed, "but you'd better watch your back. You're going to end up dead before we can put you back in jail."

Elam raised his eyebrows. "Is that a warning or a threat? Right now, it looks like I need to watch my arm, not my back."

She let go, and he shook out his arm for emphasis. Not that it was tingling from loss of circulation or anything.

"Stay. Away. From. Lacey." Rightcross punctuated each word with a jab to his sternum. "Is that clear enough for you?"

"As a mountain stream." He gave her a jaunty salute as he retreated to the Suburban.

"Don't worry about DOSA," said Angelo when Elam climbed in behind him. "They have nothing on us. Even if they did, Dad's lawyers would run circles around them. We'll head to your motel, then back to the house." Angelo turned to the driver without waiting for a reply. "Go ahead. I'll report in." Then he bent over his phone, thumbs flying.

Elam stared out the window and gathered his thoughts. Rightcross evidently knew enough about de Goma—Diaz's—organization to consider it dangerous. DOSA must be recruiting Lacey, and the local team was tasked with keeping her out of trouble. Were the Bandidos trying to recruit her also? It wasn't a big leap to make, considering Diaz's opinion on diversification. Were Angelo's motives in appearing friendly sinister as well? The boss had said he wanted to maintain the contact. Elam had assumed the gang's primary focus was drug dealing, but maybe there was more to it. He would have to keep his ears and eyes open.

Chapter Five

Several days went by with nothing remarkable occurring. Every morning, Elam conferred with Diego, Diaz's head of security, on the day's itinerary and pertinent security measures. He had to surrender his new phone to be scanned, and he was checked for bugs. Every morning. Even though he lived in a wing of the house designated for live-in employees. Talk about thorough.

The rest of the day, Elam shadowed Diaz. The man had a nondescript office building downtown with bland cubicles, average-looking employees clacking away on computer keyboards, and no name or logo on anything. The only crime Elam could spot was a complete lack of interior design. The place needed an extreme makeover. Maybe Diaz should employ Julia for the job.

So far, Elam had overheard cryptic references to shipments, projects, product, and specimens in both English and Spanish. Diaz ranted about numbers, trends, and results. Maybe today would be more interesting.

Elam followed Diaz to his office on the top floor and stationed himself outside the door. He could see inside the thick, glass windows—bulletproof, he guessed—but could hear nothing. Diaz spent most of the day on his phone—his cell, not the desk phone. And Elam twiddled his thumbs. Without any IDs to check or customers to interact with, this job was even more boring than bouncing.

Later that afternoon, as he was in danger of falling asleep, a fly landed on his nose. He waved it off, but it kept buzzing around his head. Annoyed, he flattened his hand into a paddle and swatted it against a nearby table, wiping the guts onto the carpet. Jason, the stoic armed guard who shared duty with him, raised an eyebrow. Elam just shrugged.

A few minutes later, another fly appeared. Desperate for some amusement, Elam decided to capture this one. He experimented with a few different approaches and ended up just surrounding it with his skin when it landed on his wrist. From a nearby trash can, he retrieved an empty soda cup with a lid and stuck it in there to release later. Over the course of the afternoon, he'd captured half a dozen of the annoying insects.

This morbid occupation finally wrung a comment from Jason. "That's disgusting, man."

"Nothing else to do. Why's Diaz so concerned about security anyway? There's a metal detector and security downstairs. No one gets in without an appointment. What's the deal?"

"If a tree falls ..."

Elam turned to Jason with renewed interest. "The observer effect? As the sole reason for this level of protection, that indicates some extreme paranoia."

"What the boss wants, the boss gets. That's the whole point of being the boss. Don't question it." Jason clamped his mouth shut and resumed his role of statuesque oracle.

"'Unquestioning loyalty,' I get it," Elam muttered.

Jason's phone dinged, and he glanced at the screen. "Julia's on the way up."

A moment later, the elevator door binged, and Julia glided into the room with her own goon in tow. Ignoring the guards, she marched up to her father's door and tapped on the glass. He glanced up at her and waved her in, ending his call.

Jason and Tomas, Julia's guard, stepped aside to hold a whispered conversation. A weird, low buzzing noise caught Elam's ear. He picked up the soda cup. The flies were arranged under the lid in the shape of an arrow, pointing at Diaz's office. They buzzed again, and Elam nearly dropped the cup.

Then it clicked. *Fang said he had a contact who was an animal charmer. It must be Thorax, that creepy bug guy.*

Thorax was a reclusive freelancer with a deep mistrust for the system. Except for occasionally helping Prism and Fade, the skilled hacker and entomophile eschewed all things DOSA. What could have brought him out of the woodwork?

With a mental shrug, he put his concerns over the man's motives aside and studied the bug silhouettes. They were too small to carry cameras. What was Thorax trying to do?

He flipped up the little tab on the lid, and a fly crawled out. It spread its wings and buzzed angrily. Then it flew under the desk and landed next to a large, black beetle. The beetle carried a camera on its back. Elam let the beetle crawl onto his shoe. Then he returned to his post by the door. When Julia exited a few minutes later, he held the door open for her, and the beetle crawled away onto the floor. *The flies were just to get my attention.*

Julia paused midway through the door and glanced at him as if she'd just remembered he existed. "You look good in black."

"Thanks." He'd objected to the constrictive black jacket on the grounds he didn't need to conceal a weapon and instead wore black slacks and a silk button-down shirt.

She turned back to her father. "Can I borrow him for the sorority gala this weekend?"

"On Saturday?" Diaz considered her thoughtfully. "No, take Angelo. He can help you with your little project while he's there. He's been working it from another angle. I need Elam with me."

Julia shrugged. "Too bad." She sauntered out, narrowly avoiding stepping on the beetle as it scurried toward the desk. When she entered the elevator and turned around, she eyed him again.

Elam had expected some sort of "my daughter is off limits" speech when he'd taken the job, but it had never come. He wondered what job Angelo was helping with.

Diaz's secretary, who had a desk near the elevator, crossed the room and held out a tablet and stylus for the boss to sign. She took the tablet back to her desk, and Diaz returned to his phone. Besides a legal pad and a pen, the boss's desk was clear. A shredder sat in the corner, and every day he meticulously shredded his notes after taking photos of them. However, most of what he did was verbal. Hopefully, Thorax's beetle would overhear something helpful.

Jason's phone dinged again. He read the message and frowned. "That nut job is hanging out at the front door again. We'll have to go out the back. Gerardo is bringing the car around."

"Okay." That was different.

Diaz shredded the day's paper, and Jason apprised him of the situation as they walked to the elevator.

Diaz grimaced. "Something will have to be done about him."

This was obviously a rhetorical statement, but Elam couldn't help wondering what would be done. The man must be making himself a menace, but why?

When the elevator reached the lobby, instead of turning toward the front of the building, Jason led them in the opposite direction down a long hallway to a utility door. He held his phone up to a scanner, and the lock clicked. Elam had received instructions for such a scenario from Diego, so he stretched his arm to open the door, letting Jason step through and check the alley.

"Clear." Jason motioned Diaz forward and opened the car door for him.

Something didn't feel right to Elam. "Wait a minute." Diaz paused in the doorway. Elam stretched his neck, allowing his head into the alley and studied his surroundings. His senses prickled, but he couldn't put his finger on what was wrong.

"Come on," urged Jason. "We can't linger in the open."

Elam stretched his body into a wall on either side of his boss as he continued forward. Something moved in the shadows to the right. No, the shadows were moving. He grabbed Diaz around the waist and propelled him into the vehicle as a camouflaged human shape leapt forward.

Incognito!

Elam sprang into the car with the speed of a taut rubber band and slammed the door closed just as the attacker swung a machete through the space where he'd been.

Gerardo hit the gas, but he couldn't drive quickly through the narrow alley. Incognito landed on top of the car with a thump. Jason pulled his gun, but Diaz put a hand on his arm to restrain him.

"Not here, you fool," he hissed. "We're in the middle of town. Elam!"

"I'm on it," answered Elam as a wicked blade punched through the roof of the vehicle.

With one hand, Elam grasped the machete, turned it to rubber, and stretched it, pulling it into the car and dropping it on the floor. With the other, he rolled the window down and grabbed hold of a lamppost as Gerardo peeled around a corner. Keeping a foot in the car, he leaned out and swiped at Incognito, but the assassin hopped over his arm like a jump rope.

Incognito no longer bothered to blend into his surroundings. Dressed all in black, with bladed weapons strapped to his arms and legs, he looked like a cross between a ninja and a Swiss army knife. He pulled a knife from a sheath on his sleeve and threw it at Elam. Elam released his hold on the lamppost and used the extra momentum to catapult himself into Incognito as the blade flew past his ear.

They rocketed into a concrete wall and bounced off. Gerardo sped down the street, taking the boss to safety. Elam wrapped Incognito up like a roll of dimes. With one grotesquely elongated arm, he grabbed Incognito's collar and shook him.

"Who are you working for? Why are you after Diaz?" he screeched, vocal chords stretched thin.

Incognito strained against his rubber bonds but Elam held him fast. The assassin's camouflage-based powers and a minimal strength boost couldn't compete with his flexibility in a fight. However, his skill with knives was legendary in villain circles. Elam couldn't risk him getting an arm free.

"Let me go! If you knew what that monster was up to, you'd let me kill him!"

"Why don't you enlighten me?"

"As if trafficking drugs wasn't enough. He's taking evil to a whole new level."

"Says the guy who always ignores the 'alive' option for collecting bounties."

Incognito shrugged his eyebrows since he couldn't move his shoulders. "It's way easier." His eyes narrowed. "But I've never gone after kids."

The assassin glanced over Elam's shoulder and cursed. His powers blinked in and out, though it did no good. Elam owled his neck to see Rightcross approaching with Transporter, a sable with telekinetic powers. He wasn't a powerful sable, but the talent was rare enough that DOSA recruited him anyway.

Elam scowled. He'd forgotten, for a moment, that the Reno team was still dogging him. Incognito would never divulge anything now. Briefly, Elam considered loosening his grip and letting the assassin claw free, but they'd only end up right back where they were, maybe with someone getting hurt. Elam didn't know what he would do when protecting Diaz conflicted with helping Fang. He hadn't even heard from the latter since starting this gig. If not for the bug, he might have thought he'd dreamed Fang's visit.

"Well, well," said Transporter, "Villains doing our job for us. Gift-wrapped and everything."

"Since you're here," said Elam, "I'd appreciate the loan of some handcuffs."

"We're not loaning you anything," scoffed Rightcross. "We're taking over. Be glad we don't arrest you too, for disturbing the peace." She pulled out a disruptor cuff. "Let one of his legs loose so I can slap this on."

Elam shook his head, the only body part that was currently its normal shape. "His power isn't what's dangerous. He's armed to the teeth. The disruptor won't affect his knife-throwing ability."

Rightcross pursed her lips. "Okay, I think we have some of the old-fashioned kind in the van."

"I know where they are," said Transporter. He hustled around the corner.

Rightcross turned back to Elam with an odd expression.

"What?"

"I've never actually seen you … like this. It's kind of disturbing."

"Glad I could make an impression."

Transporter returned promptly. "Since I knew where they were, all I had to do was open the door and I could summon them."

"Way to go, Errand Boy."

Transporter gave him a withering look.

"Boy Errand? Gopher Boy?"

"Just hurry up," snapped Rightcross. "The sight of you is making me sick. In more ways than one."

It took some contortions on Elam's part, but eventually the three of them got Incognito cuffed and disarmed. Rightcross added the disruptor for good measure. "I don't want him blending in and trying to get sneaky," she explained.

Elam nodded in agreement. "Incognito," he appealed to the man again, "is there anything else you can tell me?" He'd felt that the assassin would have divulged some important information if they hadn't been interrupted.

"What's the point? You've gone soft. Turned into a dirty stool pigeon. I'm not talking to you or anyone else."

"Enough." Rightcross took Incognito by the elbow and jerked him forward. "Let's go."

"Hang on, Rightcross," said Elam. "I assume, since you're not questioning me or giving me a hard time, that you must have been keeping an eye on me?"

"Is that a surprise?"

"No. I just wanted to say thanks."

"Okaaaaay." Rightcross raised an eyebrow.

"And I'll pass on a tip. Keep an eye on Lacey this weekend, especially if she goes to the Sorority Gala."

Both eyebrows crept higher. "How do you know about that?"

Elam put up his hands. "Hey, that's all I'm saying. See you around." He stretch-leaped down the block and headed back toward the Diaz mansion.

Even though they didn't know about his undercover mission, having Rightcross and Transporter around to back him up turned out to be a good thing. Maybe DOSA was good for something after all.

Chapter Six

When Elam entered Diego's office, the head of security sat grilling Jason while Angelo lounged against the wall behind him.

"Bentley, you made it." Elam wasn't sure where he'd served, but the man obviously had a military background and called everyone by their last name. He also had a distinct Puerto Rican accent. "What happened?"

Elam related the events. Angelo tapped away at his phone while Diego studied Elam intently.

When he finished, Diego grunted. "Too bad DOSA picked him up." He cracked his knuckles. "I would have liked to interrogate him myself. What do you know about him?"

"He's an assassin, responsible for pretty much every high-profile, unsolved murder involving knives. He has no particular vendetta that I know of. Someone has to have hired him or put out a bounty on Diaz."

Diego nodded as though unsurprised. "That's why we hired you, to fend off sable attacks. Though you," he wagged a finger at Jason, "should still have noticed the distortion in the shadows."

Jason shifted uncomfortably.

"What about the 'nut job' hanging out at the front door?" asked Elam. "Was he involved in some way?"

"No," said Diego gruffly. "We know who he is."

Diego's tone indicated the subject was closed. Elam felt he needed to keep digging. He'd been here over a week and had discovered nothing helpful. Plus, Incognito's attitude had disturbed him.

"I said Incognito had no vendetta that I know of in his past cases, but he said something that made me wonder if he had a more personal motive this time."

Diego leaned forward. "What did he say?"

"He said he'd never gone after kids."

At this, Diego stiffened. Behind him, Angelo pushed away from the wall. "Thank you for your quick action today," said Angelo. "My father will be grateful."

"Yes," said Diego. "You may resume your duties. You will find Mr. Diaz in his study. It will be best if you do not repeat anything that assassin said."

Elam stood, knowing he'd touched a nerve. Had a child been hurt by someone in Diaz's network? Was a family member avenging an overdose victim or a gang hit? Elam had no evidence of anything. He didn't even have proof that Diaz was a gang boss or drug trafficker at all. All he had was Incognito's cryptic remark and what Fang had told him. He could accuse Angelo of attempted murder, but that would never stick.

Somewhat frustrated, he made his way to Diaz's study. The boss sat rigidly at his desk, peering at his cell phone. When Elam entered, he set it down and smiled. "Elam, you have earned your salary today. I appreciate your alertness and quick response. Angelo has given me a full update. You will find a substantial bonus in your weekly deposit."

"Thank you, sir." According to his first paycheck, he was earning two thousand a week just for standing around. What would Diaz consider 'substantial'? His DOSA pay, to be set aside for him until the undercover work was over, was hardly worth remarking on, though double-dipping was awesome.

Diaz waved him aside, and Elam took his normal post until Diaz retired for dinner, at which time Elam was relieved. He ate his own dinner in the kitchen before retiring to the staff lounge. The room was empty, but the TV was on. Elam flipped to the news. When they got to local headlines, an anchor stated that notorious supervillain Incognito had been apprehended by the Reno DOSA team. They showed a brief clip of Rightcross and Transporter leading the villain into headquarters with Byte waiting for them at the door, and then the topic switched to sports. That was fine. Elam didn't need to be mixed up with it. But he had hoped there would be more information about Incognito's recent activities. He needed a lead.

With his phone history scrutinized every morning, Elam had to be careful what he searched for online. However, he had accounts with several dark web sites with secure access that even Diaz's people shouldn't be able to hack. He retreated to his tiny, spartan bedroom to do some searching. If anyone questioned him, he could say he was researching supervillain activity in the area so he would know what to look out for.

As soon as he logged in, his message board lit up. He clicked on the anonymous message.

Rubber Bandit, a five million dollar bounty will be paid to your account upon the execution of Julio Diaz.

Five million dollars! It was enough to make anyone adjust their loyalties. His weekly paycheck looked like chump change now. Who could want Diaz dead that badly and why? That was the entirety of the message. Elam logged out, set his phone down, and leaned against the bedframe. If he turned on Diaz, would anyone from the Bandidos seek revenge? He bet Angelo would. The kid clearly had a crazy streak. Who knew what kind of precautions Diaz had taken for such an event. He'd have to hide out somewhere, probably eastern Europe or Asia.

With a sigh, he stared at the ceiling. Who was he kidding? Killing people wasn't his thing. Even if he wanted to become a hit man, which he didn't, he knew better than to attempt anything without a solid exit plan.

Seeing movement out of the corner of his eye, Elam glanced at his window. A giant stick bug clung to the screen. It looked like something was attached to its body. With a shudder, Elam opened the window and pushed out the screen, catching it before it could fall. By rubberizing it, he maneuvered the screen inside the window without bending it and set it on the foot of the bed.

The walking stick rotated in a circle, letting Elam examine the gear it carried. On its back was a camera and what looked like an earpiece. Carefully, Elam released the tiny Velcro strap holding the earpiece and placed it in his ear.

"Hello?" he said tentatively.

The bug bent its legs to adjust the angle of the camera.

"Hello, Bandit," Thorax's voice crackled in his earpiece. "I can't exactly say I'm pleased to work with you since you threw my catch phrase in my face and attacked my friends the last time I saw you."

"I seem to remember you sent a swarm of bees after me, so I think we're even," Elam replied dryly. "We'd better make this quick. Diaz's people are constantly sweeping for bugs." He cringed at the unintended pun. "They could detect your signal at any moment."

"Not *this* signal. Their tech gurus have nothing on my skills. Besides, we don't need to talk long. DOSA has sent Sonical out to help. He'll be listening in on everything from now on."

Elam tapped his chin in thought. He'd never met Sonical, though he'd heard of him. His skills were more useful behind the scenes than in a fight, though he could reputedly manipulate sound waves with devastating effects. The dude could hear through walls from a mile away. Elam hoped they were set up discreetly in a nearby house and not an obvious vehicle.

"Does he speak Spanish? Probably half the conversations here are in Spanish."

"No, but he doesn't have to. This guy is incredible," Thorax's voice took on a fan-girl quality. "All he has to do is open his mouth, and his vocal chords replicate the sounds he's hearing. Then I just record it and run it through a translator."

"There has to be a lot of sound here. That would be pretty noisy." His mind filled with kitchen and bathroom noises, not to mention cars.

"He can focus on one conversation. Listen, there's a lot of talk about a shipment arriving Saturday. You've got to make sure you're with de Goma when he goes to inspect it."

"You can't just follow him and raid the warehouse or whatever?" Elam kept his voice low. The TV blaring in the lounge would keep anyone in the common area from overhearing him.

"No," Fang's voice came over the speaker, "we have to know what it is and if there's enough evidence to tie de Goma to it. We can't have him claiming ignorance and getting off. We need someone on the inside."

"I can't wear this earpiece all day. Someone will notice, even if they don't detect the signal. How will I know what to do?"

"You'll have to play it by ear," said Fang without irony. "Just stick with de Goma, and restrain him if necessary. Keep anyone from getting hurt."

"Speaking of getting hurt, what about the bounty on him? What if other supervillains come after him?"

"Same thing. Just do what you've been doing. The local team is still keeping tabs on you. We'll read them in when necessary, and there are other DOSA agents in the area, ready for a raid. My department is on standby to deal with all the non-sable gang members."

"About that, I still haven't heard anything that ties him to anything illegal. No one has even used the name de Goma. I expected gang bosses would flex their muscles a little more."

"They're still building their base here in Reno. For a long time, Reno and Vegas were controlled by the mob. Now they're controlled by the Nevada Gaming Commission."

"Yeah, the government has to regulate everything," muttered Elam.

"The criminal element has turned to illegal drugs to make their money," continued Fang. "While a gambling addiction can have a devastating effect, drug overdoses are spiking out of control. We have to do something to stop it."

Elam had no desire to have a conversation on which vices were worse than others. He had more practical concerns. "What if I need to get ahold of you guys?"

Thorax broke in. "The earpiece has an on/off button. When it's off, there's no signal. Turn it on, and I'll know. You can talk, and Sonical will hear you. We'll reply. I've got it all set up now, and he has a lock on your voice, so you can let my phasmid out."

"Your what?"

"The stick bug."

"Oh." Gingerly, Elam replaced the screen, and the walking stick slowly wandered off. "Did you get anything from the beetle in Diaz's office?"

"Not much. The guy has code names for everything. Like, he said he was excited to see more of Botero's work, but he didn't find Khalo as inspiring. And he planned to get rid of his Zeduan."

"Weren't they artists?" Elam felt he should get the reference, but this was not his area of expertise.

"Yeah. Your detective here thinks it relates to drug sources, but that doesn't help us much."

Elam heard whispering in the background.

"Hey, the Hedgehog here says someone's coming, so we gotta bug out," said Thorax. "Turn off that earpiece and hide it somewhere."

Elam yanked the earbud out and pushed the tiny button on the side. The green light faded. For now, he stuck it in his pocket. Firm footsteps sounded in the lounge, heading toward his door. Knuckles rapped on the wood.

"Bentley."

Elam jumped up to open the door for Diego. "Yes, sir?"

"You got an extra job tonight. Angelo's gotta go out, and Diaz wants you with him."

"Okay." Great. Elam's least favorite person. What kind of job would Angelo need help with? If his services were required, it had to be something that couldn't be taken care of with only a gun. The thought was not comforting.

Chapter Seven

Elam followed Diego to the foyer where Angelo was waiting with Carlos, the guard he'd knocked out the first night. The kid wore a suit coat this evening, and Elam noticed the bulge of a holster.

Angelo nodded at him. "I've got a little problem to take care of. You won't need to do much, just watch my back."

"Can do."

"Perfect. And don't worry about your DOSA shadows. They've already left for the evening."

The local office didn't have the staff for around the clock surveillance, so that meant no backup from Rightcross or Byte. Somehow, it made him feel alone to know they weren't nearby. He slid his hand into his pocket and pushed the button on the earpiece. Even if he couldn't put it in his ear, it should alert Thorax that something was going down.

Angelo got in the front with an unfamiliar driver, and Elam climbed in back with Carlos. They rode toward town in silence. Elam hoped Thorax and Sonical were able to follow him. Unless the sable could track a specific engine through traffic, he supposed they'd need a voice to follow.

"Normally, Diego briefs me on where we're going, but he didn't prep me for this." Elam glanced from Angelo, whose thumbs flew across his phone, to Carlos. After their auspicious introduction, he and Carlos hadn't spoken much. "Anything I need to know?"

Carlos stared straight ahead, refusing to acknowledge him. After a short pause, Angelo answered without looking up from his phone. "It's possible I may need you to demonstrate your skills for some of my friends." He turned his head and met Elam's gaze with one eye. "That won't be a problem, will it?"

"As long as you don't ask me the same way you did last time." Elam tried to project casual bitterness. Was that a thing?

"I won't, but someone else may," answered Angelo evenly. "You should stay on your toes."

"We follow orders," put in Carlos gruffly, "and our orders are to protect Angelo and do what he says."

"Thanks for the clarification."

They pulled into the parking lot of a fancy casino. Elam followed Angelo and Carlos into the building while the driver kept the car running. They rode the elevator to the top floor where Carlos knocked on the door of a high rollers suite. No attempt was made to avoid cameras. Elam assumed Angelo expected to get away with whatever he planned to do.

A man in a Tang suit opened the door, and stood aside to let them enter with a sweeping bow. They entered a large suite decorated with Chinese paintings and calligraphy. A middle-aged man in a silk robe sat in an armchair, smoking a long bamboo pipe. Elam's nostrils flared at the smell.

A woman in a pantsuit stood to one side. Her dark hair was pulled back into a tight ponytail. Obviously security, Elam studied her objectively. No gun. The man who opened the door retreated to the far side of the room and put his hands inside his sleeves. Probably had throwing knives hidden there. Carlos positioned himself between the doorman and Angelo, so Elam moved to his other side.

"Xiàngpí Fěi." Angelo tipped his head toward the man in the chair in a slight bow.

"Angelo, isn't it? De Goma's son? Would you like a *yen tsiang*?" The man held out a second pipe.

Elam hoped Sonical was listening, since this was the first reference to de Goma he'd heard so far.

Angelo shook his head. "It is my father's policy to keep a clear head."

"That is wise." He motioned for Angelo to take a seat. "What can I do for you?"

Rather than take a seat, Angelo stepped closer to one of the paintings to inspect it. "It has come to my father's attention that you have broken your agreement."

Xiàngpí Fěi set his pipe down on a stand and steepled his fingers. Angelo turned to gaze at him. "I assume he is in no doubt of his information since he sent you in his place."

"Your inferior product continues to flood the market after multiple warnings. You were to pull out of Nevada or pay us a percentage. I have come to collect." Angelo's tone remained even while his words grew menacing.

Elam studied the room for hidden threats. The row of glass windows on the far wall had lines of sight to several nearby hotels and casinos. A barbell stood propped in a corner with a stack of heavy weights next to it. A baby grand piano filled another corner.

Xiàngpí Fěi tilted his head back. "We agreed to that arrangement only because you had a distinct advantage at the time. Now we would like to renegotiate. Split the town down the middle. You take the east side of town; we'll take the west."

"Have you not heard about our newest product line, then?"

The man in the robe frowned. "New product? You mean a new source? People don't care as much about quality as they do about price. They'll use an inferior blend at the risk of their own lives if it's all they can afford." He indicated his pipe. "That's why I prefer more traditional forms of recreation." With an air of complete unconcern, he stretched out his feet. "They can go to your side of town if they want something more refined."

"Not a new source." Angelo's eyes lit, and he leaned forward on his toes, "an entirely new form of revenue. One that will eventually give us control of the entire west coast. Perhaps the country."

Chills ran up Elam's spine at Angelo's words. The kid's face glowed with pride. Something about him was just creepy and made Elam nervous. What could they have that could compete with the powerful west coast crime syndicates?

"Indeed." Xiàngpí Fěi leaned forward and raised an eyebrow. "And what is this new product?"

Angelo shook his head. "If you don't play by the rules, you don't get in on it." He pulled himself up to his full height. "Do you have our payment?"

Xiàngpí Fěi picked up his pipe again and took a puff. "I think not."

Angelo turned to Elam and gave a nod.

Rather than attack Xiàngpí Fěi whom he felt was no threat, Elam's arm shot forward to grab the woman. At the same time, she stretched her hand toward the barbell, and it flew into her palm.

A metal manipulator with magnetic powers!

He wrapped his arm around her waist and tried to reel her in, but she swung the barbell with her free hand and hit a coffee table, flipping it toward him. He dodged the table, quickly grabbed the barbell, and rubberized it.

The weights lifted from the floor and shot toward him, one after the other, like frisbees. He ducked, tugging the woman with him. Instead of crashing into the wall behind him, the weights changed course midair as the woman waved her arm like a conductor directing an orchestra. Angelo dove for cover as one barely missed his head. One hit Carlos in the shoulder as he grappled with the doorman. Elam rolled aside as one thudded into the carpet where his head had been. Then the woman grabbed the air, and the weight slid across the floor and bashed him in the hip.

If she has magnetic powers, her arms must be polarized. He had to keep her from using them. Releasing her waist, his arms wrapped around hers just as she reached toward the piano. An odd creaking noise rose from the instrument as thick wires snapped free and snaked toward him. He tightened his grip and tried to lower her arm and turn it to rubber, but she resisted. For some reason, her body didn't respond to his powers.

A wire coiled itself around his neck. Even when elasticized, his air flow could be cut off. His grip on her arms weakened, and his vision blurred. Though he tried to rubberize the wire, it continued to tighten. He didn't have much time. She had to be stopped—now.

Wrapping his legs around hers to steady himself, he released one of her arms and stuffed his hand in her mouth, expanding his fingers until he'd completely blocked her windpipe. She clawed at his hand, eyes wide, until finally passing out. The wire around his throat fell away, and he gasped for air. He crawled onto a nearby sofa to get his bearings.

Across the room, Angelo rose and dusted off his jacket. Carlos joined him. The doorman lay on the floor, unmoving. Xiàngpí Fěi sat rigidly in his chair, his face ashen.

"Carlos," said Angelo in a cheerful tone, "there seems to be some conveniently placed wire lying around."

Alarm bells screamed in Elam's head. This was bad. This was very bad. But his throat hurt and he struggled to breathe. Carlos tugged on gloves. "We have to get out of here," Elam rasped.

A knock on the door supported his statement. "Hotel security. Is everything okay?"

"We're fine." Angelo surveyed the room and frowned. "I guess we'll have to speed this up." He reached into his jacket and pulled out a pistol equipped with a silencer. As Xiàngpí Fěi sucked in a breath to yell, Angelo pointed the gun at him and pulled the trigger, then turned it on the woman before checking the doorman. It was over faster than Elam could open his mouth.

"Bandit," Angelo called as he fired the gun at the window. Cracks spidered across the glass. Carlos walked over and knocked the glass loose with his gloved hand.

It took Elam a moment to realize Angelo was talking to him. What he had seen had stunned him. He pushed himself to his feet.

"Take us down."

Elam shook his head to clear it. He staggered to the window, the fresh air sharpening his senses. "It's a long way. I'll have to let you down one at a time." Talking was painful.

"Fine." Angelo wiped the gun of prints and dropped it in front of the sable. "I'll go first."

Elam wrapped his arm securely around Angelo and lowered him from the window. He had to hang onto the frame and stretch his whole body to reach the pavement.

"We're coming in," warned security.

He deposited Angelo safely below and snapped back into the apartment to fetch Carlos. Once he had lowered the guard, he released his hold on the window and fell to the pavement just as the door swung open. His frame quivered like jelly at the impact, but he bounced back quickly.

As soon as all three were in the car, the driver took off. Angelo resumed his texting. A police cruiser passed them, sirens wailing, headed toward the hotel.

"Did you know they had a metal manipulator?" asked Elam.

"I'd heard rumors." Angelo glanced at Elam over his shoulder. "You need to watch your tone."

"I don't like being surprised. I asked you if there was anything I needed to know. You should have told me the rumors."

"Unquestioning loyalty, remember? That's what you agreed to. You responded well, with no further warning. You did a great job. Don't ruin it."

Elam threw himself back into his seat and fumed. He'd started the fight at Angelo's request. Sure, he'd subdued the woman. But he wouldn't have killed her, not if there had any other option. He'd thought he was just supposed to give a demonstration of his abilities. How could he have been so naive? Gangs and drug dealers were a whole different type of criminal than he was used to dealing with. Most of his jobs had been heists or bounties, working alone or with maybe one or two other supervillains. Nothing like *this*. Nothing this *cold*.

He shuddered. Should he have stopped Angelo? Could he have? It had taken him a minute to recover. Another second and Elam would have been the one dead.

Maybe I should have dropped him from the window.

But that wouldn't have been professional of him. It wouldn't have solved anything—it would only have made Fang's work harder. At least, no one had said his name until afterwards, and he hadn't spoken during the fight, so there was little to incriminate him personally if all DOSA had was sound. However, getaway drivers had been sentenced to prison for less. Fang had better have his back with this undercover stuff.

Regardless, he was not going to be a party to any more executions. Especially of other sables just doing their job. The woman had shown incredible skills. Elam realized Angelo hadn't drawn his weapon until after he'd knocked her out. He could never have fired his gun if she'd been able to use her powers against him. No wonder they'd needed him tonight. He was going to have some choice words for Diaz in the morning.

But first, he needed to rest. He was sore and exhausted. He raised his hand to run it through his hair and stopped, remembering where it had been. Before he could rest, he would have to wash. Too bad he couldn't wash away his regrets.

Chapter Eight

The next morning, Elam woke to a loud knock on his door. His alarm beeped.

"Bentley, the boss wants to see you in his office. Now. We're heading into town later than normal. Same routine."

Elam glared at the door, slaying Diego with his thoughts. *Man, what I wouldn't give for laser powers right now.* "On my way."

He threw on a clean set of clothes, grateful he'd showered the night before, and made his way to Diaz's office. A guard opened the door for him before he could throw it open. He marched into the room and stood before Diaz's desk, hands clenched at his sides.

Diaz glanced up at Elam and nodded at Jason, who stood by the wall. Jason flipped a switch and a second set of lights turned on. Purple lights. Elam's body tingled and his powers receded. *A disruptor light!* He'd heard about them, but never seen one.

"Take a seat," said Diaz with a hint of amusement. "We need to talk."

Shaking and weak, Elam slid into a chair. It felt like the same chair he'd sat in before, but it had been reupholstered. All the things he'd wanted to say fled his mind.

Diaz stood, walked to the front of the desk, and bent down to bring his face to Elam's level. "Do you think I would have hired you without taking precautions? You saw last night what happens to people who don't follow my rules. While having you on my team makes things much easier, there are other ways to get around sables. Angelo reports that you questioned him." Diaz leaned forward until he was within an inch of Elam's face. His calm voice chilled Elam to his core. "I don't like that."

Elam gripped the arms of the chair. This guy was scary. He wanted to respond, but his tongue stuck to the roof of his mouth. All thoughts of ditching Fang and giving Diaz his full loyalty fled. He would run at the first opportunity. If he could get away with it, he might even rethink his "alive" policy on bounties.

Diaz searched Elam's eyes intently before straightening. "I see you are afraid. That is good. A healthy dose of fear will keep you in your place. I assume you will have no more questions?"

Elam shook his head. "No sir," he forced his wooly tongue to form the words.

"Good, good. Because you are too valuable an asset to eliminate unnecessarily." Diaz opened a desk drawer and drew out a disruptor cuff and a remote. The guy had some good connections to enable him to procure all this restricted tech. "As it is, you will wear this." Diaz shoved the cuff across the desk. Jason unclasped his hands, giving Elam a better view of his gun. "Put it on."

Fuming, Elam took the cuff and attached it to his ankle. Diaz tossed the remote to Jason. "If another super-abled attacks us, Jason will deactivate the cuff. And just in case you're thinking of running, or if you fail to do your job," Diaz flipped open a folder and slid it toward Elam. "It could put others in danger."

Elam glanced down at the folder. Photos of Thirsty and his regulars, Lacey, the Reno DOSA team. Diaz was reaching. Good thing Elam didn't have many friends. The ones he did have, he'd kept away from on purpose. He shoved the folder back. "What makes you think I care about any of these people?"

Diaz nodded slowly. "I think you do. Your history shows you avoid causing collateral damage. You recently intervened in a robbery to save a child you didn't know. Though you turned a few people over to some unsavory criminals for ready cash, I have yet to uncover a case of you killing anyone personally. You have a soft spot, Rubber Bandit. If the thought of these people suffering fails to move you, we can find others. I am tracking down a name as we speak."

Diaz turned his legal pad around. At the bottom of the page was written Hortencia Garcia. Elam's jaw tightened.

"You've hidden her well, but we will find her. This woman is like family to you, yes?"

Elam glared at Diaz, again wishing his eyes could shoot lasers. "Where did you get that name?"

"I, too, have contacts in Colombia. I have checked you out thoroughly." Diaz smiled, obviously satisfied with himself. "I like being able to hold things over people's heads. It's too bad we couldn't pin last night's crime on you. You handled Angelo's gun the other day, but your fingers are too stretchy to leave prints. But persuasion is kind of a hobby of mine. I can always find a way to get what I want."

No wonder someone had it in for the guy.

"Don't worry." Diaz leaned back in his chair. "As long as you follow orders, there will be no problem." His stare turned icy again. The man reminded Elam of a broken thermostat. "Are we going to have a problem?"

"No, sir." Elam was in over his head. There was nothing he could do.

"Very good. Let's get going."

***

To Elam's surprise, Julia joined them for the morning drive. She wore a tight skirt and a blue satin blouse, open to show a small necklace with a clear, circular locket holding several charms and a lot of glitter. The childish piece of jewelry looked out of place on her smooth, caramel skin.

Diaz patted his daughter's knee. "You look perfect. Are you ready?"

Julia smirked. "Absolutely. This should be fun."

Elam had a sinking feeling that whatever they had planned would not be fun at all.

When they pulled up to the office building, an unkempt man in jeans and a T-shirt stood holding a sign that read, JULIO DIAZ IS A KIDNAPPER. He flipped it over, and the other side read, WHERE IS HALIE?

What is that about? Elam wondered. *This must be the 'nut job' they were talking about yesterday.*

"What do I do?" asked Elam. Again, Diego's briefing had been lacking in details.

"Stay back and watch for supervillains," said Jason from the front seat. "Make sure this guy doesn't run off."

"Otherwise, don't interfere," warned Diaz. He scooted out of the Suburban and opened the door for Julia. They walked toward the building together with Jason right behind.

Elam scanned the nearby offices and the street but saw nothing unusual. A few people walked along the sidewalk. Cars drove past. It was business as usual.

"Where is my daughter?" yelled the man with the sign. "Your business is a front for drug dealing and human trafficking." He held up a phone and shouted into it. "This man lures children into slavery. He hooks them on drugs."

A bystander paused and pulled a phone out of her bag. She pushed a button and held up the camera as the man continued.

"I demand justice. He—" the man broke off as Diaz and Julia walked right up to him. The man stared at Julia. He lowered his phone and dropped his sign, pointing at Julia's necklace. "Where did you get that? That's Halie's necklace."

He lunged for the locket. Rather than back away, Julia leaned into the man, and he tripped over her foot, grabbing her arms to steady himself.

Julia screamed. "Help! Assault! This man is groping me!"

"What?" said the man, straightening. "I didn't do anything!"

A police car conveniently drove around the corner and pulled up to the curb as they argued. An officer got out. "What's going on?"

"He assaulted me!" Julia pointed at the protestor.

The bystander held up her phone. "I saw the whole thing. He definitely groped her."

"I didn't!" he exclaimed.

"I'm pressing charges," huffed Julia. "I insist you arrest this man. He broke my necklace, too." She held out a locket similar to the one she had been wearing, but Elam was sure a couple of the charms were different. "You can take this as evidence."

Over the man's profuse and loud declarations of innocence, the officer handcuffed him and stuffed him in the back of his cruiser. "I'll need to take down your information," the officer said to Julia and the bystander, who Diaz must have planted. "A detective will be in touch to get your full statement."

Once the officer left, Diaz's party entered the building and stepped into a meeting room.

"Excellent job, my dear," smiled Diaz. "You were perfect."

Julia half-closed her eyes in a smug smile. "It was easy." She put her hand inside her shirt and pulled out a second necklace. "Here's the real one. The magnetic clasp worked like a charm." She giggled at her pun as she held it out.

"Thank you, sweetheart." He kissed her cheek as he pocketed the bejeweled bait. "You should probably show up at your classes today."

"At least I'll have a great story to tell everyone. They'll all know how distraught I am." She put a hand to her forehead and feigned faintness. "Too bad Angelo had to miss it."

"Yes," agreed Diaz. "But it was best for him not to go out today."

"I'll go home and update him later. *Chao.*"

Elam felt disgusted. These people were terrible. There was no longer any doubt that it was a family business. Evidently, the people Diaz trusted most to do his dirty work were his own children. How could Elam take him down without anyone he knew getting hurt in the process?

Julia left, laughing maniacally, and Elam and Jason accompanied Diaz upstairs.

"Good to have that taken care of," Diaz remarked as they exited the elevator. "This is going to be a great day."

"Yes, sir," agreed Jason.

Diaz eyed Elam. "Don't pretend to have some sort of righteous indignation against my tactics. You know what happened to Vellum. You're responsible for that."

Elam froze. He'd turned Vellum, a sable with rare invisibility powers, over to a French-Canadian villain called *Onde de Choc*. Later, he heard she'd been electrocuted. At the time, he'd needed the money and hadn't thought much about the consequences, but he'd felt bad when he discovered what had happened.

"And Grand Adventure Vacation Investments went bankrupt after your heist," continued Diaz. "The CEO committed suicide."

Elam's throat constricted. He hadn't known that. Diaz was right. He'd hurt people, too. Some of them inadvertently, but most of the time, he knew what would happen. For the first time in a long time, he took a good look at his career choices and felt uncomfortable.

I'm such a hypocrite. I don't like people messing with me, threatening me, or shooting at me without provocation, yet I've attacked others unprovoked. Needing money is not a good enough reason to ruin someone else's life. Or end it.

He stood outside Diaz's office in sullen reflection. Diaz deserved to go down for what he'd done. But so did Elam. Deep down, Elam was scared. What if there was no way to bring Diaz to justice without going down with him? Diaz could easily have him framed as he'd done with the man on the street. Or maybe he'd found evidence to link Elam to crimes the police had missed?

What if standing up to Diaz got him killed?

Chapter Nine

Jason's phone buzzed. He looked at it and frowned before tapping the glass door. Diaz looked up and motioned him in. Jason opened the door halfway and stuck his head in.

"Those DOSA idiots are downstairs. They want to talk to Bandit here about last night."

Shock jolted Elam to alertness. If the local team was still out of the loop, they could cause all kinds of trouble for him.

Diaz considered. "Have security show them into one of the meeting rooms. They can't wander around the building without a warrant. They'll have to wait for us to bring him down. In the meantime, get Wesson up here."

"Should I call the judge's office for an injunction?"

Diaz considered. "No, we want to appear to be working with them. I don't want DOSA getting suspicious. Not right now."

Jason bowed his head and returned to his post to send a text. Elam waited on pins and needles. About half an hour later, a thirtyish man who looked like he stepped right off a cover of a men's fashion magazine, exited the elevator and breezed into Diaz's office.

"Wesson, thanks for coming." Diaz stood to welcome the lawyer. "Elam!" He beckoned him into the office.

Elam entered dutifully. "Yes, sir." He noticed the clasp of the necklace dangling from Diaz's pocket. It was horribly tempting. Could he grab it without being noticed? If he did, could he get it into the hands of someone who could do something about it?

"Wesson, this is Elam. Elam, you're to do everything he says."

"Elam." Wesson held out his hand, and Elam shook it.

Elam wondered if Wesson was his first or last name. "Pleasure."

"DOSA is downstairs and wants to question him about some crime that happened last night. Elam had nothing to do with it, though they may have evidence that puts him in the vicinity. He has no comment."

Wesson nodded, intelligent eyes sweeping over Elam as if assessing his abilities. "Got it."

Diaz turned to Elam. "Though I like to hold things over people's heads, I decide when and where to use my information. As I said, you have nothing to fear if you follow my orders. We'll let DOSA see you, but not hear you."

"Yes, sir."

"Jason," Diaz barked. Jason pulled out the disruptor remote and removed the cuff. "Wesson, bring Elam back up here when they're done. One last thought—" he held up a finger, "—if you get the opportunity, see if you can find out anything about the sable who attacked me the other day—Incognito."

"Will do."

Jason preceded Wesson out the door and Diaz stared after them. For a brief moment, no one's eyes were on Elam. He lengthened his finger into a long, thin strand and wrapped it around the end of the necklace. Rubberizing it so it wouldn't make noise, he slid it from Diaz's pocket and slipped it into his own as he followed the others from the room.

On the ride down, the knowledge of the necklace in his pocket burned in his mind, and he hoped his face wasn't turning red. Thankfully, his nerves could be attributed to the impending interview.

Wesson gave Elam directions in a clipped, methodical tone. "Keep your expression clear. Don't respond to anything they say. I'll do the talking. If there's anything I want you to answer, I'll let you know you can speak. Got that?"

"Got it."

When they entered the meeting room, Rightcross sat at the table while Byte stood fidgeting with a pen.

"Well, well, here we are again," Byte grinned. "Up to your old tricks, Flubber? I knew you'd get back in the game sooner or later."

"My client will not respond to such jibes," said Wesson smoothly as he slid into a seat. "I suggest you proceed with your questioning."

Elam sat across from Rightcross, deciding she was the best one to pass the necklace to. Since he was only here to sit in silence, he would stay alert for an opportunity to sneak it to her.

"Where were you last night between eight and eleven?" snapped Byte after reading him his rights.

"I have advised my client not to answer that question," said Wesson.

Byte laid some grainy photos on the table. Elam recognized himself, Angelo, and Jason in the hallway of the casino. "These photos show you outside a room where a crime was committed. What were you doing there?"

Wesson made a show of picking up a photo and peering at it closely. "Without analysis, it is difficult to say who is in these photos. They'll have to be verified."

Byte and Wesson went back and forth. Most of the time, Wesson merely responded with "my client has no comment." Byte was clearly annoyed. Elam began to relax and enjoy the sable's discomfiture. But when his eyes flicked to Rightcross, he found her studying him intently. Her thoughtful gaze made him squirm.

"You did a good job taking down Incognito yesterday." The compliment took Elam off-guard during a lull when Byte's frustration had forced him to take some deep breaths.

"Thanks." *Darn it! She got a word out of me.*

Wesson shot him a warning look. "Mr. Bentley will be happy to cooperate with the police in the prosecution of Incognito for his attack on Mr. Diaz." Happy, but careful, was the undertone.

"What is your job title?" asked Rightcross.

Elam glanced at Wesson, who nodded imperceptibly. "Personal security."

"And what are your duties?"

Again, a nod. "I stick close to Mr. Diaz and mitigate any threats."

Byte angled his body away from Elam as if bored, but his eyes sparked with interest. Wesson stiffened, alert for any traps.

"Do these guard duties extend to other members of the household?" asked Rightcross.

"What are you driving at, agent Rightcross?" asked Wesson.

"I withdraw the question. What do you do in your time off?"

"I advise you not to answer. The question is irrelevant."

Byte snarled and slammed his hand on the table. "We know you were there last night, Bandit! You either committed or were an accessory to murder, and we're going to nail you for it."

Wesson stood. "So far, the only pieces of evidence you have are some questionable photos. Unless you're charging my client, this interview is over."

"Not so fast—" Byte pointed at Wesson.

The door opened, and a woman handed Wesson a folder. The lawyer quickly perused its contents, a smug smile tugging at the corners of his mouth. "Actually, it appears the coroner has deemed your crime a murder-suicide." He threw the folder on the table in front of Byte. "We're done here."

"What? It can't be! There hasn't even been time—"

As Byte gaped at the paper, Elam surreptitiously pulled out the locket, stretched his arm under the table, and tapped Rightcross' knee. She jumped and glanced at him, and then quickly looked away while opening her hand. He pressed the necklace into her palm, and she closed her fingers around it while pretending to lean forward and study the paper. No one else seemed to notice. Elam couldn't help a breath of relief. *At least she's not as dense as Byte.*

In fact, her line of questioning was rather sneaky. If he'd come in without a lawyer, he might have divulged more than he should have. She threw him a curious glance as she and Byte walked toward the front doors, but Elam forced himself to look away.

"Well?" demanded Diaz when they returned.

Wesson recounted the interview. "In short, we cooperated by indulging their fantasies until the coroner's report came."

"Their office is conveniently speedy," smiled Diaz. "That's good. Angelo and Carlos can resume their normal activities."

Under other circumstances, Elam might have admired Diaz's extensive reach. After the morning's grill session, however, Diaz's foothold in the justice department inspired more fear than awe. Would he ever be able to break free of this group, even with Fang's help?

Diaz canted his head toward Elam. "How did he do under questioning?"

"Excellent. Only one slip. You'll have to watch him with the ladies."

Elam scowled. "It wasn't because she was a lady. I was caught off guard."

Wesson repeated the conversation while Jason replaced the disruptor cuff.

"Well, we'll let you off this time, but don't let it happen again," admonished Diaz.

The lawyer left, and the rest of the day passed uneventfully. As soon as Elam made it back to his room, he took the earpiece out of a drawer where he'd stowed it the previous evening, turned it on, and stuck it in his ear.

"Cody here, I mean Thorax."

Elam filed the name away but didn't comment on Thorax's slip of the tongue. "I'll make this quick. Fang needs to get in touch with Rightcross ASAP. She has some evidence relating to the scene outside the office this morning. It belonged to a girl named Halie."

"You got the necklace? Awesome, dude! I can't believe Diaz set Jim up using his own daughter. It's a new low."

"Wait—Jim? You know him?"

"Yeah, he's the reason I'm on the case. It takes a lot to persuade me to work with the authorities, but when I heard Halie's story, I knew I had to help bring Diaz down. Fang's already working on getting Jim out. This will help."

Elam had more questions, but he was running out of time. "Hey, when Diaz discovers the necklace is missing, he'll probably have me searched, so I'll have to ditch the earpiece."

"Okay. Tomorrow is the big day. Some important shipment is supposed to come in, so make sure you're there for that."

"I'll do what I can. Signing off." He ground the earpiece into pieces with his shoe, then flushed it down the toilet.

It was just in time. He'd barely started to undress when Diego burst into his room without bothering to knock. "Look everywhere. Turn everything over and inside out. Him too."

"Hey, what gives?" Elam protested as Carlos and Tomas entered and began tearing his things apart.

"Be orderly about it," said Diego. "We don't want to miss it." He turned to Elam. "Strip. Hurry," he ordered when Elam hesitated, "or we'll do it for you."

Slowly, Elam peeled off his clothing. What followed was a search akin to an airport security nightmare.

"He hasn't got it," shrugged Carlos when they had finished. "At least not here. It was too big to swallow."

Tomas jerked his chin at Elam. "Couldn't he have swallowed it using his powers?"

"With this on?" Elam pointed to his cuff incredulously.

"Even if he did, he'd have to pass it. We can check him again later. The dogs are searching the grounds; Gerardo is searching the car. It has to turn up." Diego turned to Elam. "For now, you're confined to your room. I advise you to comply."

"Sure. It's past my bedtime anyway. I should sleep like a baby after this."

Angelo appeared behind Diego. "Anything?"

"No. Jason didn't have it either?"

Elam couldn't help a smug satisfaction that he was not the only one subjected to such indignities.

Angelo shook his head. "Nope. I had my money on Elam here."

"After this morning's lovely chat with your father, you think I'd do anything to get on his bad side?" Elam scoffed. Fortunately, being a criminal with a secret identity made him a good liar. Even if the person he lied to most often was himself. "Can I put my clothes back on?"

The goons filed out of the room. Elam donned his pajama bottoms and pulled a T-shirt over his head to hear Diaz raging.

"Where is it?" He marched up to Elam and grabbed a fistful of his shirt fabric. "What did you do with it?"

"What did I do with what?" Elam looked down at the much shorter Diaz. The man's normally imperturbable expression was livid. His eyes bulged and his cheeks were red. Elam thanked whatever instinct had led him to get rid of the earpiece.

"The necklace, you imbecile! Don't pretend you didn't take it."

If Elam had learned one thing in his life, it was that if you repeated a lie often enough, people believed it. "I didn't take the necklace. Last I saw, you put it in your pocket."

"Are you saying I lost it? I do not lose things."

Elam put up his hands. "I'm not saying that at all. I'm just saying that's the last time I saw it."

Diaz let go of his shirt with a shove. "When I find it, whoever took it will be a dead man." He stalked angrily out of the room.

Elam let out a long breath once Diaz had gone and he was finally alone. He flopped onto his bed and stared at the ceiling. After the last two days, he felt a little shaky. Not to mention, the disruptor was painful. Sharp, needle-like pulses of energy penetrated the skin around his ankle. At least he only had to wear one. DOSA had put one on each limb and one around his waist. He stretched out an arm to touch the ceiling. The parts of his body away from the disruptor still responded. Good thing the gang didn't fully understand the tech they were using.

With a sigh, he turned out the light but doubted he could sleep. Diaz had been more worked up than he'd expected. Whoever Halie was, her case must be significant. Hopefully, Diaz would cool down by the morning and take Elam with him to view the special shipment that was due. He recalled Diaz's words about righteous indignation.

The jerk was trying to manipulate me into believing I'm no better than him. Maybe I'm not now, but I can change. I'm not going to give in or go along with this villain. I'm not going to be paralyzed by guilt, either—I'm going to do something!

He sent up a prayer to whatever god was listening that he'd find a way out of this mess.

If I make it out of here alive, I'm going straight. No question about it. Even if DOSA is the only option.

Chapter Ten

Diego woke Elam early to inform him Rightcross and Transporter had stopped by to give Diaz a head's-up that another supervillain had come to town.

Elam groaned. "Who is it this time?"

"Stokehole. Heard of him?"

"No, but I assume he has fire powers." Elam shook his head. "That's a horrible handle."

"Yeah." Diego had no sense of humor. "Said he used to hang out with some villainess named Jupitress."

"Oh." Elam blinked. No wonder it was such a terrible name. Rightcross had made him up. He would have remembered if Jupitress had a friend called Stokehole. Fang must have let the local team in on the operation, and Rightcross had come to ensure Elam would be along.

"Diaz wants you five minutes ago." Diego snapped his fingers repeatedly to encourage him to hustle.

Elam dressed hurriedly and rushed to the study.

"—You sent her flowers, right?" Diaz was asking.

"Of course," answered Angelo. The two of them stood talking in the middle of the room.

"Make her feel sorry for you. You've never had a chance, you need her to save you—"

Angelo nodded. "I remember what to say. This isn't my first time."

They looked up as Elam entered.

"Ah, Elam." Diaz clasped his hands behind his back. "I am going to give you an opportunity to prove your loyalty to me. The disruptor lights require too much power to be portable, and it appears there is another supervillain in town. I have important business in Las Vegas this evening I can't afford to miss. You're going to ride along to make sure I don't miss it."

"Yes, sir." Elam stuck out his ankle.

"Oh, we're not removing the cuff." Diaz waved toward Jason. "Jason will have the remote. He'll remove the disruptor at the first sign of trouble."

"What if he's busy?" growled Elam. "Or they take him out first?"

Diaz shrugged. "I guess we'll hope that's not the case. Get something to eat. We leave in an hour."

Elam's stomach felt tight, and he had a hard time finishing his breakfast. The bit of conversation he'd heard unsettled him. It sounded like they planned to manipulate someone, maybe Lacey. He didn't know exactly how Sonical's powers worked, but he hoped he'd been listening in.

If DOSA sent Rightcross in with that message, it must mean they are ready to take him down.

That meant Elam had to be ready, too.

***

The ride to Vegas was anything but comfortable. Except for a brief stop in Tonopah for lunch, they traveled straight through a whole lot of nothing. There was no reason to keep a lookout. The car had satellite internet, but Diego had confiscated his phone. Diaz made a few cryptic calls, but he spent most of the time sending messages. Jason stared out the window as if the desert scenery mesmerized him. Elam almost stretched his fingers and tied them into knots before he remembered the disruptor. He didn't want to give away the fact he could still manipulate his other limbs.

Late in the afternoon, Carlos pulled the Suburban up to a large warehouse in a Las Vegas industrial park. Elam didn't recognize the logo on the outside. They waited outside a loading bay until the door slowly rolled up, and they drove in.

"Carlos, stay here with the boss while Elam and I check it out," said Jason.

Elam got out of the car. His eyes adjusted to the dim lighting. Crates, pallets, a forklift, and numerous boxes lined the walls, but in the center was a passenger bus. A black stretch hummer sat next to it.

"Jason," called a man behind them.

Elam whirled around to see a burly man in casual clothes walk toward them from the door control panel as it lowered.

"Hunter," replied Jason. "Did you have any trouble?"

"Nope. Smooth sailing. Pete and I took turns driving and resting, so we only stopped for gas and food." He whistled, and another man exited the bus. "Pete" opened the luggage compartment and dragged a man in handcuffs out of it. He grabbed the man with one hand and a suitcase with another.

Elam's chest tightened as he recognized the second man. It was Sebastian. The man who had injected him with sable serum. What was he doing here? Elam's pulse spiked as he tried to remember if they'd had any conversations about Hortencia and his mom. Had he let a clue to their location slip? Is that why Diaz had brought him here—to try to track down Elam's friends and family? He shook himself and made a show of walking around the stacks of crates.

Maybe Diaz doesn't know our connection. I have to play it cool.

Pete and Sebastian stood waiting while Jason and Elam searched the rest of the warehouse. Sebastian glanced at Elam but had the good sense to keep quiet.

When they had finished, Jason returned to the Suburban and pulled a semi-automatic rifle from the back. Elam went cold. Things just got more serious.

Jason tapped on the window. "All clear."

Diaz got out of the car.

"Keep an eye out for sables," said Jason. "I'll stick with Diaz."

Elam nodded, hanging back as Diaz beelined for Pete. He enlarged his ears imperceptibly as Diaz spoke in low, rapid Spanish.

"So, you are the scientist who has had such success creating unauthorized sables?" Diaz eyed Sebastian up and down.

"This is him," said Pete when Sebastian didn't answer. "The coyotes who smuggled him in verified his identity. We have his ID, and the gang who picked him up for us ransacked his lab and sent all his samples and downloaded his notes." Pete wore a smirk, as pleased as if he'd done it himself.

"Excellent," said Diaz. He gestured toward the suitcase. "Is that what this is?"

Elam had glued his eyes on the high windows and the doors, but now he rotated slowly to keep the suitcase in his periphery.

Pete nodded. "That's everything that was left after we injected the assets."

Assets? Now Elam was totally lost.

Diaz waved Jason over. "Open it," he ordered.

Jason set his rifle on the crate, took the suitcase, and set it next to the gun. Swiftly unzipping it, he flipped it open to reveal a small, hard case and several binders. He unlatched the case, and inside it were vials and syringes.

Diaz leaned in and frowned. "They don't have to be kept cold?"

Pete shook his head. "Evidently, the serum is shelf stable."

As Diaz inspected the content of the case, Elam's mind raced. *What does he want with the serum? He said he didn't want to be a sable, so he isn't going to use it on himself. What does this have to do with narcotics? Is he going to replicate and sell it? Is that his drug diversification plan?*

When Diaz appeared satisfied with the contents, he motioned everyone toward the bus. Jason picked up his rifle but kept it pointed down. He didn't seem to fear whoever was inside. Elam noticed Pete and Hunter both carried pistols in holsters like Jason and Carlos did. Nervously, he listened for sounds outside, but heard nothing. Where were Fang and DOSA? If they were listening, he had to give them a clue what they were walking into.

"How much firepower do we have?" he asked Jason as they followed the others.

"Plenty." He chambered a round. "Why?"

"Just wondering how powerful that sable Stokehole is."

"With as many guns as we have, it doesn't matter." He eyed Elam. "We probably don't need you. You're here just in case."

"That's foooooor sure," said Elam, emphasizing the 'for' and hoping Fang would get the reference.

Hunter opened the accordion door and climbed the steps, and the others followed.

What Elam saw inside flabbergasted him. Over a dozen children of various ages stared back at him, strapped down with disruptor cuffs. Over half of them looked Hispanic, but a few darker and paler faces hid in the shadows. Now Elam understood what Incognito meant about Diaz and kids. He was creating his own army of sables. That was his idea of diversification: superpowered human trafficking. Horror froze him in place.

Diaz hopped into the bus and walked up and down the aisle, inspecting the 'cargo.' He grabbed one boy by the chin and turned his face toward him. "Yes, you will do very well." As he walked back to the front, he paused by one of the older girls, and she shrank away from him. "You have been a lot of trouble. I hope you will be worth it."

He turned and addressed the group with the air of a tour guide. "Welcome to the Bandidos, dear ones. Don't be scared. You are joining a new family. I will take care of you like a father as long as you are obedient children. You have had plenty of food, yes?" he placed a hand on a child's head.

"We will be testing you over the next few weeks to see what powers you will develop and how we will train you."

Diaz turned around and locked eyes with Elam. "You will have an essential part in this training. Your skills will be useful."

Over your dead body!

"How am I supposed to train a dozen children by myself?" he growled, nauseated by the audacity of this man.

This is bad. This is really, really bad.

Diaz gestured toward Sebastian. "Your friend here will help you." He peered at the scientist. "How soon can we expect the children to exhibit their powers?"

Sebastian shivered and shook his head. "I don't know. It has never been tried on children before. Usually, children develop their powers around twelve or thirteen. Some of these children are younger. There is no telling how long it will take. And sometimes, it doesn't work at all."

Diaz exited the bus and sauntered over to Sebastian. "It had better work. I chose you because you have had the best results with the formula outside of DOSA. I have followed your work." He gestured toward Elam and hardened his expression. "It would be too bad if we had to discard any unsuccessful experiments."

A girl whimpered, and Diaz narrowed his eyes. "Transfer them to the limo for the ride to the ranch."

Adrenaline surged through Elam's system. His blood pounded in his head. He had to do something. He hoped DOSA was nearby, but even if they weren't, he'd wait until the children were in the limo and drive off with it. Vegas being one of the only places a limo would not be remarkable.

"I'm ready," he said to anyone who was listening.

A tremendous bang made everyone spin around as an enormous metallic humanoid cannoned through the door, leaving a gaping hole. Jason, Hunter, and Pete lifted their firearms and emptied their magazines at the intruder, but the sable held up a hand and the bullets fell to the ground.

Screams rose from the bus, and Elam ran toward it and shut the door, his first thought to keep the children safe. As the metal manipulator ripped the guns away from the thugs, Pete sped toward the bus. Before he could yank the door back open and climb in, Elam shot out an arm and grabbed Pete's leg, causing him to slam against the concrete floor. Then he grabbed the keys from the man's hand so no one else could drive off with the children.

Diaz sprinted toward the Suburban as Carlos revved the engine. Carlos rolled down the window and pointed his gun, but the metallic sable stretched out his hand and it flew into his grasp. Elam threw his arm around Diaz like a lasso as DEA and DOSA agents poured into the building. The remaining thugs were quickly apprehended. Elam picked Jason's pocket and used the remote to remove his disruptor while Jason gave him a death glare.

Through the sea of uniformed agents, Elam noticed Fang, who met his gaze and headed toward him.

"Good work, Elam. Thanks for letting us know what we were looking at. Your comments helped us decide to send in Decimator first."

Diaz squirmed in Elam's grip. "You think you can keep me locked up? You can't pin anything on me! I have powerful connections. I have the entire state of Nevada in my pocket! No one will convict me."

Elam had seen Diaz's reach first hand. He feared the man's threats were true. Decimator and a speedster joined them as Elam released Diaz's arms so Fang could handcuff him.

"Everything seems secure," said the speedster. "We're calling in backup to help with the kids, but we'll have to be careful removing their disruptors in case any of them exhibit uncontrolled powers." She shook her head as officers opened the bus door and began unstrapping the children from their seats. "This is just awful."

"If they're from out of the country, it will take us a while to reunite them with their parents. Parents who may not be equipped to help them adjust," said Decimator.

"This is way worse than anything I had imagined." Fang grimaced, shaking his head. "Well, we'll take Diaz and his men in for processing. Thanks for your help."

"I'll be out before tomorrow morning," hissed Diaz. "My lawyers will run circles around you, you sad little detective."

Something clicked in Elam's brain. With lightning speed, he flipped open the case of serum and grabbed a syringe. He popped off the cap, jabbed the needle into Diaz's shoulder, and emptied the contents into the muscle.

"Ow! What do you think you're doing, you traitor? I'll have you brought up on assault charges!"

Elam ignored Diaz's bluster and turned to the DOSA agents. "Now he's a sable. DOSA has jurisdiction, right?"

The agents gaped at him. Then a slow smile spread across their faces. "Yes, that's true. We'll take him back to headquarters and ensure he's brought before a federal judge in DC."

Diaz snarled in anger and threw his elbows as they each grabbed one of his arms. "You'd better let me go if you expect to see Lacey Greenberg again. She'll be a dead woman if you don't release me immediately."

Fang cocked his head at the man. "You mean the Lacey Greenberg who just helped catch Angelo Diaz in an attempted kidnapping?" He glanced at his phone. "The Reno DOSA team is taking her home right now."

Diaz howled with rage as the agents hauled him out of the building to a waiting vehicle.

"Diaz was blackmailing Greenberg into letting him use his warehouse and doing favors for him, threatening his family if he failed to comply," explained Fang.

I bet Greenberg is the one who put the bounty on him then. He did not voice the thought aloud. "Did you find out about the necklace girl, Halie?" he asked instead.

Fang nodded. "The necklace was a prototype for a new line—one of a kind. The one they gave to the police was similar, but not the original. Diaz had to keep it safe because it was easily identifiable. We believe Angelo enticed the girl into a vehicle on a pretext. I hope she's one of the ones here."

"That would mean she's been experimented on."

"Unfortunately. The effects of dosing someone her age are unknown. They'll all have to be under observation for a while." He glanced at the case with the serum and back at Elam. "However, Diaz is right. He can press charges against you for injecting him, and that could jeopardize the whole operation. I'll have to talk to our legal team to figure something out."

Elam winced. "Sorry about that. But I just couldn't let him wriggle out of this. It wasn't an empty threat. He does have a panel of judges and police on his side. I've seen it."

"I know." Fang nodded. "We're working on that. You've given us the best chance we could have. I understand the serum isn't effective on everyone."

"I hope he gets snail powers. The guy is slimy." Elam smiled wryly. "I'll do the time for assault if I have to. Diaz has to be put away." He shuddered at the thought of being shut inside a sterile, white DOSA cell again.

"Let's hope it won't come to that. Come with me, and we'll get your statement."

Elam filled in the gaps in the sound surveillance. Hours later, he was finally able to go home—or back to the motel in Reno. He wasn't sure if it was a good or bad thing that his previous room was still available. Once he'd closed the door behind him, the tension of being undercover relaxed. Though some of the supervillains he'd worked with in the past had been violent and volatile, none of them had been as diabolical as Diaz.

For a minute, he'd actually considered screwing DOSA over and sticking with Diaz—the easy job and good pay tempted him—but he and Angelo were too temperamental. They scared him, and not much did that.

Plus, what they were doing was plain sick. Incognito was right, messing with kids crossed the line.

Elam showered, threw on a T-shirt and boxers, and flopped onto the bed. What was he going to do now?

Chapter Eleven

The next morning, Elam woke slowly and stared at the ceiling. The bright cracks of sunlight around the heavy motel curtain hinted dawn had long passed. There was absolutely nothing he had to do. He might as well stay in bed.

He reached for the remote and turned on the television. After flipping through the channels and finding nothing interesting, he turned it off in disgust. Maybe he could call Thirsty. With the Bandidos out of the picture, the trouble at the bar would be over and he could go back to work.

While he considered this, a sharp knock sounded on his door. Had Fang come with news about the assault charge? Or an update about Halie? He threw off the covers and bounded out of bed, yanking the door open without looking through the peephole.

Rightcross stood there with a hand on her hip, raising an eyebrow at his minimal clothing. He ran his fingers through his disheveled hair and willed his face not to flush.

"Well ... You're still here. Fang said you would be. I half thought you'd skip town."

"How could I live without my shadows?" He peered past her. "No Byte to your bark today?"

She rolled her eyes. "Get dressed. We need to take a walk."

Elam swallowed. This was it. Back into DOSA custody. Well, he promised Fang he'd do whatever it took to keep Diaz behind bars. "Okay, just a minute."

He shut the door and dressed quickly. When he opened the door again, Rightcross stood staring at her purple fingernails.

Her gaze flicked down to Elam's pink hightops. "Nice shoes."

"Thanks. Can we get this over with?"

She jerked her head toward the shabby pool chairs. "Over here is fine."

Elam frowned as he followed her to a table in the shade. "You're not taking me in?"

"What's your hurry?" She cocked her head at him. Then she smiled. It was a nice smile. He wasn't sure if he'd seen her wear one before. "Before I take you in, we need to discuss terms."

Elam was lost. "Terms? What do you mean?"

Rightcross relaxed into her chair. "Let me back up. You royally flubbed up when you dosed Diaz with serum. He wants to press charges." She held up a hand to forestall his protest. "I know it was the only way to get him into DOSA custody, but his charges won't stick if someone in our pay is convicted of assaulting him. Fortunately," she grinned, "You haven't received a paycheck from DOSA yet."

A light came on. "But I did get paid by Diaz ..."

Rightcross leaned forward and nodded. "If you're not connected to DOSA, we can't help it if one of his own men turns on him."

"What about the deal I signed?"

"What deal?" She smirked. "I never saw it. And neither will anyone else."

The corner of Elam's mouth twitched. "I seem to remember you heroes aren't great at paperwork, not even the electronic kind."

"It's one of my professional improvement goals this year. That's one of the differences between heroes and villains—when we screw up, we get more paperwork, when you screw up, you go to jail."

Elam stiffened. Without DOSA protection he could be charged as an accessory. "So ... why are we sitting here then?"

"Because, I'm here to offer you another option."

"You mean ..."

"I mean, join my team through the Supervillain Rehabilitation program."

Now it was Elam's turn to raise an eyebrow. "Your team? What about Byte?"

"He's taking a desk job in DC. DOSA wants to expand the Reno team, so I'll be rebuilding almost from scratch. With a brand-new facility, by the way, thanks to a substantial donation from Greenberg Enterprises. I'll have Transporter, Sonical and his translator, and I want you."

So, even though Diaz came out alive, Greenberg must be satisfied to be rid of him and have Lacey safe. Did DOSA know he'd put out a hit on the guy? Hopefully, the donation came with no strings attached.

Elam considered Rightcross's offer. The idea of being wanted for a team affected him more than he would have expected, but he tried not to show it. The sense of family he'd felt with Thirsty and the guys at the bar had given him a taste of a life he hadn't had since he was a kid. Even being part of Diaz's gang had been better than being alone.

"Why me?" he rasped, throat suddenly dry. "I've been a villain for so long. Why not some squeaky-clean doe-eyed idealist?"

Rightcross shrugged. "Better the devil you know. I've seen you in action, and I like your skill set. I'd rather have someone who's comfortable with his powers than a newbie. What do you say?"

Something she'd said came back. "What do you mean, Sonical's translator? Not Thorax?"

"The bug guy? No. He's gone back off grid. He wasn't really working for us. Halie's dad hired him—"

"Was she there?" Elam interrupted.

A softness crept into Rightcross's expression. "Yeah. She was there. She's home now."

The tension in his chest eased. The girl would likely have some major trauma to deal with, but at least she was home with her family. His eyes glazed over as he thought about having a place to call home. He hadn't had that in years.

Rightcross cleared her throat, bringing him back to the present. "Anyway, Sonical is … a special case. You'll be intrigued by his skills."

Interesting. He'd thought all they had to do was hook Sonical up to a recorder.

Whatever. That wasn't important.

Should he tell Rightcross about his mom and Hortencia? Would he be able to visit them?

"So, how does the SVR program work exactly?"

That bright smile spread across her face again.

"Let me tell you."
                        The End

ABOUT THE AUTHOR

Amber Gabriel is a Central Texas artist, author, and teacher. Scribbling since she was old enough to hold a crayon, she drew her first (unsanctioned) mural at the age of five, inspired by the eminent painters Glip and Glop of Richard Scarry fame. In order to keep an eye on her, Amber's artistic mother set up a canvas and easel on the dining room table.

Since then, Amber has completed many commissioned artworks, including portraits and large outdoor murals. As her first mural was inspired by a
book, it should be no surprise that she also writes medieval action-adventure romance and contemporary fiction for both children and adults.

While most of her creative talent is focused on planning incredible lessons for her students, she still writes and draws as often as possible.
Read more at https://authorambergabriel.com/.

Also by Amber Gabriel:

The Edge of the Sword, adult kingdom adventure

The Lost Bride of Verda (prequel novella)
A Crack in the Rock
Seven Years in Shelomoh (companion novella)
The Warrior Prince of Berush
In Search of Magic Fire
The Throne of Cerecia
The Princess of Everywhere
Captain of the Sand

Middle Grade Fiction

The Junk Drawer Adventures
I & the Magic Pen
I & the Scaredy Cat

Christian Romantic Suspense

Frame of Reference

Anthologies:

Wags, Woofs, and Wonders

DOSA Files

DOSA Files II

Seasons of Romantasy: Spring

ABOUT THE PUBLISHER

Born in a small town in north central Oregon, H. L. Burke spent most of her childhood around trees and farm animals and always accompanied by a book. Growing up with epic heroes from Middle Earth and Narnia keeping her company, she also became an incurable romantic.

An addictive personality, she jumped from one fandom to another, being at times completely obsessed with various books, movies, or television series (Lord of the Rings, Star Wars, and Star Trek all took their turns), but she has grown to be what she considers a well-rounded connoisseur of geek culture.

Married to her high school crush who is now a US Marine, she has moved multiple times in her adult life but believes home is wherever her husband, two daughters, and pets are.

For information about H. L. Burke's latest novels, to sign up for the author's monthly newsletter, or to contact the writer, go to:

www.hlburkeauthor.com

Books by H. L. Burke

For Middle Grade Readers

Thaddeus Whiskers and the Dragon
Cora and the Nurse Dragon
Spider Spell
Absolutely True Facts of the Pacific Tree Octopus

For Young Adult Readers

An Ordinary Knight
Beggar Magic
Coiled
Spice Bringer
The Heart of the Curiosity
Ashen

The Nyssa Glass Steampunk Series:

Nyssa Glass and the House of Mirrors
Nyssa Glass and the Juliet Dilemma
Nyssa Glass and the Caper Crisis
Nyssa Glass's Clockwork Christmas
Nyssa Glass and the Electric Heart

The Dragon and the Scholar Saga (1-4)
A Fantasy Romance Series

Dragon's Curse
Dragon's Debt
Dragon's Rival
Dragon's Bride

Other Fantasy Romance

To Court a Queen
Match Cats: Three Tails of Love

Ice and Fate Duology

Daughter of Sun, Bride of Ice
Prince of Stars, Son of Fate

The Green Princess: A Fantasy Romance Trilogy

Book One: Flower
Book Two: Fallow
Book Three: Flourish

Spellsmith and Carver Series

Spellsmith & Carver: Magicians' Rivalry
Spellsmith & Carver: Magicians' Trial
Spellsmith & Carver: Magicians' Reckoning

Fellowship of Fantasy Anthologies

Fantastic Creatures
Hall of Heroes
Mythical Doorways
Tales of Ever After
Paws, Claws, and Magic Tales

Supervillain Rehabilitation Project

Relapsed (a short story prequel)
Reformed
Redeemed
Reborn
Refined
Reunion

Blind Date with a Supervillain
On the Run with a Supervillain
Captured by a Supervillain
Engaged to a Supervillain
Accidentally a Supervillain

A Superhero for Christmas
A Superhero Ever After
Second Chance Superhero
Wishing on a Supervillain
Her Fake Superhero Boyfriend
Rescuing a Supervillain
Courting a Superhero

Power On
Power Play
Power Through
Power Up

Game On
Coming Soon: *Game Changer*

The DOSA Files Anthologies:
Volume I
Volume II
Volume III

Made in the USA
Coppell, TX
07 May 2025

48977785R10062